CAI

ANNA STONE

CHAPTER 1

The most beautiful woman Tess had ever seen just walked into Cherry's Diner.

As she wiped down a table, the woman strode toward a booth in the corner and took a seat. *What's someone like her doing in a place like this?* Cherry's was a sketchy little diner in an even sketchier part of the city. And the food? In the four years since Tess started working here, it had only gotten worse.

But no one came to Cherry's for the food. They came to Cherry's because it was the only place in the neighborhood that was open past midnight. Or because they were lost.

Necessity, bordering on desperation. The only reason anyone set foot inside the diner. And that was the only reason anyone worked there, including Tess. After graduating from high school and getting kicked out of her foster home, she'd needed a job. Cherry's had been the answer. Without money, an education, or any family, what else was she supposed to do with her life?

But the woman who just walked in? She was different

from everyone else in the room. She didn't seem desperate, although there *was* a chance she was lost. She looked completely out of place.

It wasn't only her sophisticated manner that betrayed her. The clothes she wore were finely tailored, her knee-length black dress so snug on her hourglass figure that it had to have been made for her. Her heels were the same ink-black as her dress, as was the wide-brimmed hat she wore, despite the late hour. Her hair, a dark chestnut brown, flowed from underneath it, partially obscuring her face from view.

But a glimpse was enough for Tess to see how beautiful the woman was underneath. *Beautiful. Elegant. Sexy as sin.* The kind of woman Tess only dreamed about. With all the time she spent waiting tables, she daydreamed constantly. About escaping this place. About starting a new life, one that wasn't a never-ending grind to pay her bills.

About someone sweeping her off her feet and taking her away from it all. Someone like the woman who had just walked in.

But she never allowed herself to indulge in those dreams. She was never going to escape her situation, not by her own power or anyone else's. Life didn't work that way. Not *her* life, anyway. Ever since her mom died when Tess was ten years old, she'd been left to struggle through everything on her own. That wasn't going to change anytime soon.

"Are you okay? You've been wiping the same spot for like five minutes."

Tess blinked. Ashley, one of her coworkers, was standing next to her, a stack of dirty plates balanced in her arms.

"Right." Tess straightened up. "I was just distracted."

"By that woman?" Ashely cocked her head toward the booth in the corner. "I don't blame you. Even *I* think she's hot, and I'm not into girls. I didn't know anyone could look like that in real life. I hope I look that good when I'm her age."

"Yeah." Everything about the woman was so flawless that it was hard to tell how old she was, but she seemed to be in her thirties, forty tops. "What do you think she's doing here?"

"Who knows? She's in your section, but if you'd rather just stare at her all night, I'm happy to take her off your hands. I bet she gives good tips."

"I got it." Tess didn't want to miss her chance to talk to the woman, even if it was just to take her order. "I need all the tips I can get."

Ashley shifted the plates in her arms. "What do I keep telling you? You gotta smile more. And flirt a little."

"You think she's into women?" Tess could only hope.

"It doesn't matter if she is or not. Men, women, they all like it when you flirt with them. People love attention, no matter who it's from. It makes them feel big. Important. God knows anyone coming to a dump like this needs that."

But that only worked for people who looked like Ashley. She was platinum-blonde and had the kind of figure men and women alike drooled over.

Tess? While she cleaned up well, she was no bombshell. Her hair was the plainest mousy brown imaginable, and her skin kept forgetting that puberty was long over. Occasionally, she got compliments on her eyes, which were a vivid shade of blue.

3

"Flirt a little," she repeated. "I'll try."

"Well hurry up," Ashley said. "If Cherry sees you standing around, she'll dock your tips again."

That was the last thing Tess needed right now. She barely made enough to cover her rent and bills as it was. The fact that her boss considered labor laws a suggestion didn't help.

As Ashley headed toward the counter, Tess took a deep, steadying breath. *Here goes nothing.*

She strode over to the woman's booth. "Hi there."

The woman raised her head, giving Tess a clear view of her face. Dark eyes, sharp and piercing. Graceful cheekbones, crimson lips. Around her neck was a delicate string of pearls.

Were they real? Who would wear pearls to a place like this? It was like wearing a sign that said 'rob me.'

But something told Tess that the kind of opportunistic thieves who roamed the streets in this part of the city wouldn't dare approach this woman. She radiated a coldness that Tess could feel in the air around her.

And she wasn't the only one. Even the other diners, the hardened regulars, barely looked in the woman's direction. Were they intimidated by her?

Tess remembered herself. "What can I get for you?"

The woman didn't answer her immediately. Instead, she looked Tess up and down, her penetrating gaze making Tess's skin burn.

When she finally spoke, her voice was smooth and low, commanding enough to send a shiver through Tess's body. "Coffee. Black."

Somehow, Tess managed to keep her cool. "Anything to eat?"

The woman tilted her head slightly, her eyes still fixed on Tess. She hadn't touched the menu in front of her. "What do you recommend?"

"I'd go with the waffles. Honestly, most of the food here is terrible, but the waffles are actually good." Cherry would do more than dock Tess's pay if she overheard that. But this woman seemed to have good taste. Tess couldn't lie to her. And a part of Tess felt compelled to please her.

"Waffles it is." The woman glanced at Tess's name tag. "Thank you, Tess."

Her cheeks grew hot. "I'll be back right away with your coffee. Let me know if you need anything."

She hurried back to the counter to put in the woman's order before returning to pour her a cup of coffee, almost knocking over the pot in the process. And she nearly tripped over her feet as she walked away.

So much for Ashley's advice. Tess could barely speak to the woman. Flirting was beyond her. Why was she so flustered? All because of a beautiful woman?

But Tess didn't have the time to obsess over her. Because only a minute later, a large, rowdy group of men walked into the diner. Or rather, stumbled in. Chances were, they'd been kicked out of the bar across the road. Or the strip club nearby.

They made a beeline for Tess's section, spreading themselves out across two tables.

"Not going to offer to take these guys off my hands?" she muttered as she passed Ashley.

"Nope. You're on your own."

Tess sighed. "It's going to be one of those nights, isn't it?"

Sure enough, within minutes she was so busy dealing with the group of drunk men that she didn't get another chance to speak with the woman outside of serving up her waffles and topping up her coffee.

It wasn't until an hour later, when the men had finished shoveling down their meals and were out the door, that she noticed the woman was gone. She'd left before Tess had even had a chance to give her the bill.

Tess frowned. Had the woman run off without paying? That seemed unlikely, given how rich she appeared to be. But it wouldn't be the first time she'd gotten stiffed by a 'wealthy' customer.

She approached the table. The woman had polished her plate. And tucked underneath it was a handful of bills.

Tess lifted the plate. On top of the bills was a napkin, the words 'Keep the change' written on it. She picked up the money. They were fifty-dollar bills.

And there were five of them.

Holy...

She counted the notes again. $250. Were they counterfeit? They looked real. Maybe the woman had made a mistake. The meal was barely $20, after all.

Tess blinked. She was standing in the middle of the diner holding up $250 cash in full view of everyone! What the hell was she thinking?

She stuffed the money into her pocket. But it was too late.

"Shit!" Ashley sidled up beside her. "That's a hell of a tip. What did you do to get that?"

Tess shook her head. "I don't know. Maybe it was a mistake."

"Don't look a gift horse in the mouth, girl. That's more than I've made this week."

Tess glanced around. No one else had noticed anything. But her boss, Cherry, was behind the counter, talking to one of the other servers.

Everyone at Cherry's, customers and workers alike, was like Tess. Desperate, broke, and struggling to make ends meet. If they found out Tess had gotten a $250 tip? They'd find a way to take it from her.

"Please don't tell anyone about this, okay? I don't want people to get jealous. And I don't want Cherry to come up with an excuse to steal it from me." She reached into her apron pocket where she kept her change. "Here, I'll give you twenty dollars to keep quiet."

Ashley snatched the bill from Tess's hand. "It's a deal. And just so you know, I wouldn't have told anyone, anyway."

But Tess wasn't taking any chances. While she'd known Ashley for years, and even spent time with her outside of work on occasion, her coworker's loyalty was to herself and herself alone. If the payout was high enough, she'd sell Tess out.

From behind the counter, Cherry barked at the two of them to get back to work. As Ashley hurried away, $20 richer, Tess cleared the corner booth.

Why did she leave me all that money? Tess had no way of finding out the answer. She didn't even know the woman's name. She couldn't track her down to thank her, or ask her why she did it. Chances were, Tess would never see her again.

At least, not outside her fantasies. Because from the moment she'd walked through the door, the woman had set up camp in Tess's mind. *Beautiful. Elegant. Commanding. Sexy as sin.* Everything Tess had ever dreamed of and more.

And she had swept in and out of Tess's life like a cold winter breeze.

CHAPTER 2

It was 3 a.m. when Tess finished her shift. After saying goodbye to Ashley and the others, she left Cherry's Diner and began the walk back to her apartment. At this time of night, the streets were deserted, save for the occasional cab looking for a late-night fare. Despite how much her feet hurt from standing for eight hours straight, she couldn't justify the cost of a cab. And the walk was only half an hour.

But this wasn't the safest part of town. A couple of years ago, she'd had her tips stolen while walking home from work one night. Since then, she'd carried a can of pepper spray with her in her jacket pocket. She hadn't had to use it yet.

She glanced around. She didn't usually have so much money on her. Maybe she should have sprung for a cab, just this once. But she was already halfway home, so there wasn't any point.

Home. For Tess, home was something that had never been more than a vague concept. As a child, she and her mom had moved from town to town, city to city, one trailer or run-down apartment to another. Her dad had never been in the picture. Tess didn't even know if he was alive or dead. Her mom had refused to speak of him, and she'd taken his identity to the grave when she died twelve years ago.

With no family to claim her, Tess had bounced between foster homes for almost a decade. The places she'd stayed in ranged from adequate to outright abusive. But even the best of them never felt like home. How could they, when they were always temporary?

The apartment she'd lived in for the past four years was an improvement. It was barely habitable, but it was *hers*. And that was more than the *nothing* she'd had most of her life.

She crossed the road. She was just a few minutes from her apartment building. But as she turned a corner into a quiet street, the sound of footsteps behind her reached her ears.

Her pulse sped up. Was someone following her?

She glanced over her shoulder. Sure enough, there was a man several yards behind her, walking in her direction. He was dressed in all black and was twice her size. In the dimly lit street, she could barely make out his face. But she could make out a menacing glint in his eyes...

You're imagining things. He's not following you. But something about the man was setting off alarm bells in her head. And life had taught her that her instincts were rarely wrong.

She picked up the pace. Was the man a customer from the diner who had seen the tip she'd gotten and was determined to take it from her? Two hundred and fifty dollars might as well be a million to someone down on their luck. Tess would know.

Just stay calm. Try to lose him. Could she rush to her apartment and barricade herself inside? No, the last thing she wanted was to lead this stranger back to her home.

It would be safer to stay out on the street where there was more of a chance of someone driving by in case anything happened. The surrounding streets were deserted, but she could take a detour through a more populated area. Maybe that would be enough to make him give up and leave her alone.

But as she crossed the street, she noticed another man walking toward her from the opposite direction. He too was dressed in all black and looked about six and a half feet tall, twice her weight in muscle. The two men were together. They had to be.

And they were coming right for her.

Tess's heart began to pound. What did they want from her? Her tips? Something else? No amount of money was worth getting hurt over, or worse. But it was better to avoid confrontation in the first place.

She turned quickly down an alleyway, a shortcut to the busy main street. If she was fast enough, she could lose the men in the alley.

Tess broke into a run. But she didn't get more than halfway down the alleyway before she heard the heavy thump of boots behind her. And they were getting closer.

Shit! Still running as fast as she could, she reached into her jacket pocket, feeling around inside it…

There!

She pulled out the can of pepper spray and swiveled

around to face her pursuer, pointing it at him with trembling hands. "Leave me alone!"

But the man didn't stop. He continued to march toward her, a hand reaching into his jacket—

Tess pressed down hard, firing a stream of pepper spray at the man's eyes until the can ran dry. He yelled out in agony, stumbling backward, his hands clawing at his face.

Now was her chance!

But before Tess could move, the second man appeared at the entrance to the alley and began running toward her. He was holding something in his hand, but from a distance, in the dim lighting, she couldn't quite make out what it was…

Is that a gun?

Her pulse thundered in her ears, drowning out everything around her. A gun. A phone. It could have been anything. But she wasn't going to wait and find out. These men weren't kidding around.

She had to get away from them, *now*.

She flung the empty can at the man, then took off down the alley as fast as her legs could carry her. As she neared the end of it, she looked over her shoulder. The second man was still following her, and he was closing on her fast.

Finding a reservoir of strength she didn't know she had, Tess began sprinting even faster. Her lungs burned, and her legs threatened to collapse, but the street was so close—

The screech of tires echoed through the air as her path was cut off by a large black car skidding across the end of the alley.

She stopped in her tracks. *No. No!* She was so close, and now this? Who was inside the car? More men?

As if in slow motion, the back passenger-side door opened. Tess froze in place, her breath seizing in her chest.

But it wasn't a man sitting in the back seat. It was a woman.

A woman in a black dress and wide-brimmed hat.

A woman with crimson lipstick and chestnut hair.

The woman from the diner.

She locked eyes with Tess. "Get in."

CHAPTER 3

Tess backpedaled. *What the hell?*

"You need to come with me," the woman said.

Tess glanced over her shoulder at the man. He had slowed his march toward her and was lurking in the alley, shrouded in shadow. Were the men with this woman? Or had the presence of a witness made him hesitate?

"Quickly," the woman said. "Before they catch up with you."

Tess blinked. "What are you doing here? Who are you?"

"Get in the car. I won't ask again."

Why would she get into the car with a complete stranger, one who conveniently showed up when Tess was in trouble? But with those men at her heels, did she even have a choice?

She didn't have time to stand around thinking it over. She had to act *now*.

With one last glance over her shoulder, she got into the back seat next to the woman. Tess barely had a chance to close the door before the car sped off down the street.

She turned to stare out the tinted back window. As the alley's exit receded behind them, she caught a glimpse of the two men standing by the street, one still dealing with the effects of the pepper spray. Neither looked happy that their quarry had gotten away.

Tess turned back around. She needed to catch her breath, and her bearings. The car she was in was spacious and luxurious, the leather interior accented with chrome and a screen separating the back seat from the driver. It was almost like a limousine.

But it didn't matter how nice the car was. Tess had a million questions on her mind. Who were those men? Why were they after her?

Who was the woman sitting next to her?

As if reading her mind, the woman took off her hat, her deep brown eyes settling on Tess. "My name is Ava."

"Tess," she replied between breaths.

"I remember."

Of course. The diner. Tess shook her head, trying to clear it. "What the hell is going on? Who were those men? I thought they just wanted to steal my tips, but then one of them pulled a gun! I-I didn't see it clearly, so I might have just imagined it, but—"

"Listen," Ava said. "Those men can't hurt you anymore. You're safe for now."

How was Tess supposed to believe that? She didn't even know who this woman was, or why she'd rescued her. Had it been chance?

Or something else?

Tess shifted in her seat. "Thank you for helping me. Could you drop me off at my apartment?" Or maybe the police station. That would be smarter, wouldn't it? She was too panicked to think straight.

"I'm sorry," Ava said. "I'm afraid I can't do that."

Tess's pulse quickened. "W-what do you mean?"

"Your apartment isn't safe," Ava continued. "Neither is your workplace. You're being watched. You can't go back, not anytime soon."

What was this woman talking about? Was she not going to let Tess go?

"Look," she began. "I appreciate you helping me, but I'd like to get out now. Can you drop me off here?"

"I'm afraid I can't do that either."

Tess cursed internally. Had she escaped those men only to end up in an even worse situation?

She needed to get out. She grabbed the door handle and pulled. It didn't budge. But that was only because the car was moving, wasn't it?

She yanked at the door handle again, panic rising inside. "Let me out!"

"At the speed we're traveling, that wouldn't be wise," Ava said.

"Then stop the car! Let me go!"

"I just saved you. I'm not going to risk your life all over again."

"Why should I believe you? You're probably with those men!"

"I assure you that's not the case. I'm trying to help you. Those men have more… malicious intentions."

Tess stared at Ava. "How do you know that? Who are you?"

"I can't explain all that to you right now. I just need you to trust me."

"Why would I trust you? You just kidnapped me off the street!"

"If I remember correctly, you got into my car willingly."

That was it? Ava wasn't even going to try to deny it? Just what kind of person was she?

What did she want with Tess? Where was she taking her?

Tess stuck her hand into her purse. She'd thrown the empty can of pepper spray at the man, but she could still call for help—

"Give me your phone," Ava said.

Tess's hand froze inside her purse. "Why?"

"Just give it to me."

Tess hugged her purse to her chest.

"If you're thinking of calling the police, there's no point. They can't protect you. Not from those men. They won't stop until they get their hands on you."

"But why? What do they want with me?"

Ava held out her hand. "Give me your phone before I *take* it."

Tess didn't know what compelled her to obey. It might have been the thunderous command in Ava's voice. It might have been her frosty gaze.

It may have been the fact that Ava's very presence made Tess's skin hot and her body tremble.

She gave her phone to Ava, her hand shaking. *Why does she have this effect on me? Why does she make me so flustered?*

Why am I still so drawn to her?

But those feelings didn't last long. Because as soon as

Ava had Tess's phone in her hand, she turned it off, rolled down the window, and threw it out of the speeding car. It smashed against the road, shattering into a thousand pieces.

Tess cried out. "Why did you do that?"

"In case your phone is being tracked. We can't take that risk."

"Do you know how much that thing cost me? I can't afford to replace it. And my shift roster was saved in the—"

"What part of all this do you not understand?" The woman's voice was sharp enough to make Tess jolt. "You are in danger. Those men won't stop until they have you in their clutches. You are *not* going back to your job. You are *not* going back to your apartment. You are *not* going back to your old life."

"But—"

"Forget about your phone. Forget about everything."

Was what this woman was saying true? Had that man really had a gun? Had they meant to harm her, or worse?

Had Tess narrowly escaped with her life?

She wrapped her arms around herself, hot tears welling in her eyes. She was scared. She was confused.

And once again, she'd been torn away from the closest thing she had to a home.

Ava's cool, firm voice broke through her thoughts. "When this is over, none of that will matter. Your phone, your apartment, your job. You won't have to worry about any of it. I swear it."

Tess sniffed back her tears. "Once what's over? What's going on? Please, can you just tell me?"

But Ava fell silent. And she remained silent for the rest of the car ride.

By the time the car stopped, it seemed like hours had passed. However, it was still dark, so it couldn't have been that long. And they weren't too far outside the city, although the tinted windows made it impossible to tell where they were.

Ava got out of the car and opened Tess's door. Tess peered past her. In the dim light, she could just make out a small airfield. At the end of the single runway was a small plane that looked to seat only a few people.

"Come with me," Ava said.

Tess crossed her arms. If Ava thought she was getting on that plane, she was crazy!

I'll make a run for it. But the airfield looked deserted, and Tess had no idea where they were. She could try flagging down a car on the highway, but who knew how long it would take for someone to drive by. That was if Ava didn't catch her first.

Tess had nowhere to run. It was hopeless.

But she remained planted in her seat, turning to face the front of the car. She wasn't going to let this woman fly her off somewhere, never to be seen again.

Ava let out a sharp sigh. "Look. I don't care if you trust me or not. All I care about is that you *listen* to me. I saved you from those men. That should be enough to tell you that I'm not going to hurt you."

Tess glanced sideways at Ava. That was a mistake. With the woman's firm gaze on her, her deep brown eyes mesmerizing, it was impossible to look away.

"I'm not going to harm you, Tess. I'm not going to let any

harm come to you. I will keep you safe, no matter what. And if that means forcing you to come with me, I will do that. I'm *not* letting you throw your life away. Not after everything I've done to find you."

Tess's stomach fluttered. What did that mean? Why had Ava been looking for her?

Why did she have a fire in her eyes that made Tess's heart race?

"I need you to come with me," Ava said. "We have to leave, now."

"I... I'll come with you." The words spilled from Tess's mouth before she could stop them. But what else could she say? What else could she do?

Ava offered her hand to help Tess out of the car. As Tess took it, a spark of electricity flowed up her arm, crackling through her until her whole body was alight.

Why did Ava's touch make her burn so hot? This mysterious woman, cold and hard as ice, was a stranger. One who was at least ten years Tess's senior, maybe even twenty.

And there was the fact that Ava was dragging her onto a plane against her will and flying her off to an unknown destination.

Yet, as Ava pulled her out of the car, it took all Tess's strength to not collapse into a helpless puddle of desire.

Ava steadied her with her other hand, which only made Tess's knees quiver. "You made the right choice," she said, releasing Tess from her hold. "Because having Riley drag you onto the plane would not be pleasant for anyone."

She nodded toward the other side of the car where the driver stood. Tess had been so captivated by Ava that she hadn't noticed the driver emerge. Tall and raven-haired, they were dressed in a suit and cap, an intimidating stance distracting from their slight frame. Tess couldn't read what gender they were.

Riley tapped their earpiece and gave Ava a nod. "The plane is ready to go."

The driver waited for Ava and Tess to start walking toward the plane before following them closely, a bag in hand. Ava braced herself against the wind, holding onto her hat, her long dark hair blowing underneath it.

As the roar of the plane's engine grew louder, she stopped Tess with a hand on the back of her shoulder, sending a shiver through her. "Before we leave, I need you to understand something. Once we get on this plane, you'll be under my protection. I will keep you safe, as long as you obey my instructions. Do you understand?"

Tess nodded. It wasn't like she had a choice in the matter.

Her hand still on Tess's shoulder, Ava guided her to the plane. As they climbed the stairs up to the door, Tess looked back at the city lights in the distance.

Breathing in one last breath of freedom, she stepped onto the plane.

CHAPTER 4

Get Tess somewhere safe.

G et Tess somewhere safe.
It was the only thought on Ava's mind when she pulled up in front of Tess at the end of the alley. And it was the only thought on her mind as the plane touched down at their destination.

They disembarked, Ava at the head and Riley at the rear, Tess between them. No one could get to her here. And Tess couldn't run off. There was nowhere to run to.

But Ava wasn't taking any chances.

As they made their way down the airstrip, far enough from the plane that the noise of the engine was reduced to a gentle hum, Tess spoke up.

"Are we... on an island?"

"Yes," Ava said. The sun was rising now, illuminating their surroundings. At one side of the airstrip, the ocean waves crashed against the rocky shore. On the other side was the island itself, blanketed in lush vegetation. That was the direction they were heading in.

Get Tess somewhere safe.

The reality was, she'd been safe the moment they landed. The entire island was Ava's. Aside from her, Riley, and a handful of trusted staff, it was entirely deserted. Very few people knew it existed.

But Ava couldn't rest until they were secure inside the house.

They headed up a path leading inland. It was flanked by forest, wild and untamed, which slowly transformed into more manicured gardens the closer they got to the mansion.

As they reached the top of the path, the house came into view. It sprawled across the highest point on the island, rising three stories high, its ivy-covered facade looming over them.

Tess stopped in her tracks, shielding her eyes against the rising sun as she stared up at the old mansion.

"Come," Ava said. "We need to get inside the house."

"That's a house? It's huge." Tess gaped at her. "Wait, is it *yours*? Do you live here?"

"Yes. This is my home. Quickly, now."

Tess obeyed, following Ava to the front doors. Once inside, she was no less in awe of the house's interior than its exterior. But Ava didn't give her time to gape, leading her directly upstairs to the room she'd prepared.

Get Tess somewhere safe.

She ushered Tess through the door. "This is your room. You'll find everything you need inside, including clothes and sundries. If you need anything else, ask Riley. They'll be just outside your door."

Tess glanced at her surroundings. "Are you saying I can't leave this room?"

There was no point in forbidding Tess from going

anywhere, not when she had nowhere to go. But Ava couldn't have Tess wandering around the mansion unattended. The old house held too many dangers.

Too many secrets.

"I wouldn't recommend it," Ava said firmly. "Not until we've had the chance to discuss your... situation. And you need rest. You've had a long night."

As if realizing this, Tess collapsed onto the edge of the bed, eyes heavy with exhaustion.

"Get some rest. We'll talk later."

Ava left the room and shut the door behind her, leaving Riley standing guard outside it.

Tess was finally safe. For now.

Ava stood under the rainfall shower in her ensuite, washing the dirt and grime of the night from her body.

This moment had been a long time coming. She'd spent months, years, tracking Tess down. She'd gone through countless private investigators, utilized every contact she had. She'd spent weeks planning, even making arrangements to bring Tess to the mansion to stay with her if necessary.

But tonight had thrown her plans into disarray.

It wasn't supposed to be like this. She'd thought she'd have more time to prepare. For more than a week, she'd watched Tess from a distance, waiting for the right time to make a move. Then she'd noticed she wasn't the only one watching Tess. She'd had to act fast. And while Tess was safe for now, the people who were after her weren't going to stop looking for her.

And when they found her? Ava wasn't certain of their intentions, but she was sure they didn't simply want to have a friendly chat.

She turned off the shower and stepped out of it, drying herself off with a towel. It was all speculation. The people who were after Tess were as ruthless as they were powerful. How far would they be willing to go to remove her from the board? At best, she faced threats and intimidation. At worst?

They would eliminate her altogether.

As for who 'they' were? Ava had a few ideas. But she couldn't risk making assumptions. Too much was uncertain.

After all, she had only just confirmed that Tess was the right girl. She didn't look anything like what Ava had imagined. Her small frame and delicate curves. Her long wavy hair, feathery light and brown as autumn leaves. Her smile —at least the glimpse of it she'd given Ava in the diner— which spoke of a depth of experience beyond her 22 years.

Her crystal-blue eyes. So familiar.

So enticing.

When she'd first laid eyes on Tess in the diner, it had taken all her willpower to keep herself together. Not only was she who Ava had been searching for all these years, she was breathtaking. Tess had an allure about her that was somehow coy and brazen at the same time. She sparked something primal inside Ava, a desire that had little to do with why she'd tracked Tess down in the first place.

Ava wanted her. To protect her. To *possess* her.

She grabbed her white bathrobe from the hook by the

shower and slipped it on. She couldn't allow herself to entertain such thoughts. Not about Tess, the woman she'd vowed to take care of.

The *young* woman, almost half her age.

The young woman who was forbidden to her in so many ways.

Ava had one purpose and one purpose only—to keep Tess safe, just like she promised. She'd already failed at that. Tess had been through more hardship in her life than anyone her age deserved. Ava could have prevented that. She needed to make up for it.

But she couldn't confuse her need to protect Tess with anything else. The lines were already blurry enough. She would need to keep her distance.

That wouldn't be hard. Ava lived by herself in an isolated mansion for a reason. She didn't care for people. She preferred solitude. And yet, she'd brought Tess back to her home with her, brought her into her sanctuary.

But she had no choice. She'd made a vow. The time had come to keep it.

She would use her sanctuary as a fortress, keeping Tess safe behind its walls. She would find out who was after Tess, confirm her suspicions. And once she had confirmation?

She would tell Tess everything. Who was after her. Why they were after her. The truth about who Tess was.

The truth about who I am?

But there were some truths Tess didn't need to know. Things from the past that were better left there. Ava's secrets were hers and hers alone.

But as she left the bathroom, a question lingered at the

back of her mind. Was she keeping these truths from Tess to protect her?

Or to protect herself?

CHAPTER 5

"Tess?" an unfamiliar voice called through the door between knocks. "Are you awake?"

Tess groaned and rolled over, catching herself before she fell out of her narrow twin bed. But the bed she was in wasn't narrow. As she stretched out her arm to one side, it didn't fall off the end. And beneath her was a mattress so soft she could drown in it, just like the covers and the pillows stacked around her head.

She wasn't in her bed. She wasn't in her apartment.

"You are not going back to your old life."

She sat bolt upright. Had all that really happened? Had it just been a bad dream?

The knocking stopped, only to be replaced by the voice again. "If you don't answer, I'm coming in."

Tess blinked the sleep out of her eyes. "I'm up! Don't come in." She was sure she looked a mess. She'd crawled into bed still wearing her work uniform, and her hair had fallen out of its ponytail at some point in the night. She didn't want whoever was at the door to see her looking so disheveled.

Was it Riley? She hadn't heard them speak more than a few words, but the voice seemed to fit. It certainly wasn't Ava's voice, that firm velvet croon that hypnotized Tess every time she spoke. Even when Ava was forcing her onto a plane...

"It's time for breakfast," Riley said. "And Ava wants to see you."

It's morning? That didn't make sense. It had been morning when she'd fallen asleep, the harsh sun peeking through the curtains covering the large bay windows. Tess vaguely remembered getting up to use the bathroom at some point before returning to bed. It had been dark then.

Had she slept a whole day *and* a whole night?

"There are clothes for you in the closet," Riley continued. "Towels and toiletries are in the bathroom. Let me know if you need anything else."

"Okay," Tess replied. "Let me clean myself up and I'll come down."

Anything to get out of this room. She'd been far too exhausted to try to leave during the night, but she was sure Riley had been keeping watch at the door the entire time, just like Ava had said.

There was no doubt about it. She was being held prisoner.

Even if it was in the most luxurious prison she could have imagined.

She got up out of the vast bed, wriggling her toes in the plush rug beside it. The room alone was as big as her apartment. And that didn't even include the ensuite bathroom and the walk-in closet at the far end of it. With its lush decor, somewhere between Victorian and modern, and polished hardwood floors and damask wallpaper, it was as elegant as a five-star hotel suite. Not that she'd stayed in any five-star hotels before. But she imagined even the fanciest didn't live up to this.

Was all this luxury an attempt to make Tess forget she'd been brought here against her will? That she'd had her phone taken from her before being flown to a remote island under the cover of darkness? That she was trapped here, with no way to contact the outside world?

That she was being held captive, and her captor refused to tell her why?

And why was she so calm? Why wasn't she breaking down, or trying to escape? Was it shock? Was it because the reality of her situation still hadn't sunk in?

Was it because she was so accustomed to having her life torn away from her that she simply shut down and stopped caring about what happened to her, just like she had as a child?

Her stomach rumbled. Maybe it was just her hunger. She hadn't had anything to eat for a whole day now. Suddenly, breakfast seemed like an enticing prospect, even if it was with her captor.

Clothes first. Then breakfast.

Tess dragged herself over to the walk-in closet at the other end of the room and flicked on the light switch. As she stepped inside, she almost pinched herself to make sure she wasn't still dreaming. Every space was filled with clothes and shoes, covering the entire fashion spectrum. T-shirts and pants. Sweaters and dresses. Feminine flats and casual sneakers. Pajamas, exercise clothes, underwear. One drawer was full of swimwear, ranging from plain one-piece suits to extremely skimpy bikinis.

Her face growing hot, she shut the drawer, instead grabbing a cardigan from a nearby shelf. It was her exact size. And so was everything else. How was that possible? It was almost like Ava had been prepared for Tess's arrival.

But why would she be?

And how did she know so much about Tess in the first place?

There was only one way to find answers to those questions. She'd have to ask Ava herself.

Tess picked out a casual jersey dress in a deep blue that matched her eyes to go with the light cashmere cardigan she'd picked up. Not only did they fit her perfectly, but they were comfortable and soft, not to mention flattering.

Why do I care how I look? She was about to have breakfast with the woman who'd kidnapped her. After saving her life, yes, but that didn't change the fact that Ava was keeping her captive.

However, Ava was so sophisticated and put together that Tess felt the need to be too. And although she hated to admit it, a part of her wanted to look good for Ava.

Despite everything, she was just as attracted to the woman as she had been the moment Ava walked into Cherry's Diner.

She headed into the ensuite bathroom and picked up a hairbrush from the vanity, running it through her hair before tying it up in a ponytail with a hair tie she'd found nearby. The vanity also sported a dizzying range of skincare products. Tess examined them all before selecting a foaming face wash and some moisturizer that smelled like jasmine.

She looked longingly at the large shower next to her. It had a rainfall head and more knobs than seemed necessary. So did the jacuzzi tub in the corner. Tess desperately needed a shower. But she needed food more.

After washing her face, she took one last look in the mirror and headed to her bedroom door. Taking a deep breath, she opened it wide.

Riley stood in the hallway just outside the door, leaning back against the wall, arms crossed. They were dressed in a suit, but a more casual one than before. It was the first time she'd gotten a good look at Riley. With their pale skin, short, raven-black hair, and angular face, they looked entirely androgynous.

Wordlessly, Riley proceeded down the hallway, motioning for her to follow. As they headed to the grand staircase at the center of the mansion and down to the ground floor, Tess took note of her surroundings but refused to be seduced by the extravagance of the mansion. She couldn't forget that she was a prisoner. She couldn't drop her guard.

But as soon as she stepped into the dining room, all her resistance dissolved. The table was a cornucopia of breakfast foods, enough to make Tess's mouth water on sight.

And Ava? She looked even more delectable. She stood by a window near the head of the table, her back to the room. She was dressed in a sleeveless black dress and heels, nearly identical to the outfit she'd worn that night in the diner. But this time, her hair was tied up into a neat bun at the top of her head, her neck and arms bare. Her skin had an olive glow that looked golden in the sunlight.

As she turned toward the door, her gaze fell upon Tess's, dark eyes locking with hers. And for a brief moment, Tess was mesmerized. It was as if her whole body was waiting for those scarlet lips of Ava's to part, to whisper a command to her. *On your knees. At my feet.*

Be mine.

Tess's stomach rumbled audibly, bringing her back to reality. She averted her gaze. How long had she been staring?

Ava gestured toward the table. "You must be hungry. Sit. Eat."

Reluctantly, Tess pulled up the closest chair. Ava took a seat at the head of the table, leaving several seats between them. Riley stood by the door, silent as ever.

Tess glanced warily at the lavish spread. She had never been so hungry in her life. But was it a good idea to accept food served up to her by her kidnapper on a literal silver platter?

"Eat," Ava repeated, serving herself some toast as if it were just another morning to her. "I didn't go through all this trouble to bring you here just to have you starve yourself."

Tess's stomach rumbled again. What choice did she have? Carefully, she took a plump strawberry from a plate of fresh fruit in front of her and nibbled it tentatively. As the juice erupted in her mouth, she had to hold back a moan of delight. It might have been her hunger talking, but the strawberry was delicious, far sweeter than any she'd ever tasted.

She grabbed herself more fruit, along with some crepes from a platter nearby, piling her plate high. It wasn't until she'd shoveled several forkfuls into her mouth that she realized Ava had barely touched her toast. Instead, she was watching Tess.

She swallowed, almost choking on her food, and grabbed a glass of orange juice to chase it. She needed to slow down.

And she needed to finally get some answers from the woman at the end of the table, who was watching her with piercing eyes and an inscrutable expression.

As Tess set her glass down, Ava spoke. "I see that breakfast is to your liking. How about your room? Did you find everything you need?"

Tess nodded. "Everything was great."

Why was Tess being so polite? She couldn't deny she owed Ava gratitude for saving her from those men. Nor could she deny she was drawn to Ava. But Ava was keeping her captive.

And she needed to find out *why*.

"So, where exactly are we?" That was a good enough place to start. She'd work her way up to the inevitable question of 'Who the hell are you and why did you kidnap me?'

"We're on an island," Ava replied. "It isn't far from the mainland. And it isn't on any maps. That's just the way I like it."

"Right. Because you own this place. This mansion. This island. You live here."

"That's correct."

"And who exactly are you?"

"Ava Vidal." She poured herself some coffee and took a

sip. "I'm sorry we had to meet under such... unusual circumstances."

Unusual circumstances? That was one way of describing things. "What exactly are those circumstances? Why did you bring me here?"

"Because I needed to get you somewhere safe. This island is the safest place there is. The only way to get here is by plane. And you'd need to know where the island is first, which hardly anyone does."

"Is that the only way off the island too?" Tess asked.

"Yes. And I apologize for bringing you here like this. But I didn't have time to explain things. My number one priority is keeping you safe."

"Safe from what, exactly?"

"From the people who want to harm you."

Tess frowned. Why was this woman being so cryptic? "What does that mean? Who wants to harm me? What do you have to do with it? Can you just tell me what's going on?"

Ava set her coffee cup down and folded her hands on the table. "I'll tell you everything when the time is right. In the meantime—"

Tess groaned. Why was Ava being so tight-lipped?

"*In the meantime,*" Ava said, "you will stay here until all threats to you are dealt with. While you're here, I will provide you with everything you need. Food. Clothing. Anything you'd like to entertain yourself. If there's something you want that I haven't provided, just ask and I'll have it brought from the mainland for you. And you're welcome to make use of the house's ample amenities."

Tess crossed her arms. "Is that supposed to make me forget that I'm being held prisoner?"

"You're not a prisoner."

"Then can I leave?"

Ava didn't answer her.

"This is insane. *You're* insane. You expect me to just accept this? You expect me to stay here with you without questioning why? You expect me to just take you at your word that I'm in danger and you're protecting me?"

But it was like talking to a brick wall. "You will have free use of the mansion, and the island," Ava continued. "However, when you leave your room, you will be accompanied by Riley. At least, until I'm sure you won't do anything rash."

"Like what? Throwing myself into the sea in an attempt to escape?"

Ava gave Tess a look that made her clamp her mouth shut. "As I was saying, you will be accompanied by Riley at all times. You met them already. They are not only my driver, but something of a... butler."

Tess glanced at Riley, who said nothing. They were just as inscrutable as Ava.

"If you need anything or would like to speak with me, ask Riley. They can also answer any questions you have. Otherwise, you're free to do as you please, except for entering any locked areas of the house. The mansion is very old. Some rooms are in need of repairs, so they're locked for safety. And my rooms on the third floor are off limits. The only other restriction is that contact with the outside world is forbidden."

"You mean, there's no internet here?"

"It's too risky. There's a chance your electronic communications are being monitored."

"By who? Who is it that's after me? Why won't you tell me?" Tess thought for a moment. "Do you even *know* who's after me?"

"I have my suspicions," Ava said firmly. "And when I'm able to confirm them, I'll tell you. Until then, I'll do whatever it takes to keep you safe. Even if that means keeping you here for weeks." She stood up. "Now, finish your breakfast. And let Riley know if you need anything."

Her plate barely touched, Ava headed for the door. But as she stepped through it, Tess called out her name.

Ava paused in the doorway. "Yes?"

Tess wasn't going to waste her breath on questions she'd already asked. But there was one question on her mind, one piece of the puzzle, that neither of them had spoken of.

She chose her next words carefully. "You keep saying you're trying to keep me safe. Why does my safety matter to you?"

For a moment, there was only silence.

When Ava finally spoke, it was with the slightest hint of emotion, more than the woman had shown Tess before.

"Because I made a promise. And I intend to keep it."

Ava left the room, her heeled footsteps receding down the hallway, her words echoing through Tess's mind.

CHAPTER 6

The first thing Tess did after breakfast was take a long overdue shower. The second?

Explore the mansion under the watchful eye of Riley.

She'd long given up on resisting the charms of her surroundings. The old house was beautiful. It was a little run-down at parts, but that only made it more appealing to Tess.

She started in the foyer, with its sprawling grand staircase, and began working her way through the rooms on the first floor. There were lounge rooms, parlors, bathrooms, each as opulent as the next.

But after seeing one sitting room, she'd seen them all. And visiting every single room on all three of the mansion's floors would take forever.

So she wandered the house at random, exploring whatever took her fancy. The courtyard and gardens. The pool and large deck at the back of the house. The sunrooms and balconies, which made the old, dark mansion seem a little less gloomy. The gym, complete with a squash court.

All the while, she was tailed by an ever-silent Riley. Sure, they answered Tess's questions, but only those that weren't important.

"So why did Ava bring me here?" she asked.

"You'd have to ask her that," Riley said flatly.

"But you know, don't you? Please, can you just tell me?"

But they didn't respond.

Tess let out a frustrated huff. "Why won't anyone tell me what's going on?"

Riley stopped. Tess stopped with them. "Look. Ava brought you here to protect you. I can't tell you any more than that."

"Can't? Or won't?"

"*Can't*. Ava only tells me what I need to know."

Why should I believe you? She didn't trust Riley any more than she trusted Ava. But maybe trusting someone was the only way she was going to get answers. And this brooding stranger was friendlier than Ava.

Well, *slightly* friendlier. Something about Riley told her that pushing them too hard was dangerous.

As they passed the second-floor kitchen, Tess decided to take the conversation in a more innocuous direction. "Who makes the food here?" She doubted Ava had made breakfast.

"The cook," Riley replied.

"There's a cook here? Are there other staff?"

"Yes. Some housekeepers, a groundskeeper. Just enough people to keep the place running."

"Including you? Ava's driver? Do you live here?"

"Not usually. My employment with her is… temporary."

What was that supposed to mean? Why was everyone being so secretive?

Tess pushed the thought aside. "How do you get food and supplies here on the island?"

"They're flown in every few days," Riley said. "Ava has a private plane and a pilot who makes regular trips. Sometimes she picks things up when she goes to the mainland herself."

Just how far from the mainland were they? Tess had been so shaken during the flight that she'd been unable to tell how long it had taken. But if Ava could go back and forth on a whim, maybe they weren't far at all.

Could Tess somehow sneak onto one of those flights? Stow away and go back home?

To where those men are waiting for me?

Wasn't that what Ava had said? That her apartment wasn't safe anymore? But how was Tess supposed to believe Ava's words when she was keeping her in the dark about everything? How was she supposed to accept her situation without knowing what was going on?

Tess didn't know if she was safe here. She didn't know whether to stay put or try to escape. But she needed to do *something*. At the very least, she needed more information, more insight.

She turned to Riley. "Who is Ava, anyway?"

"She's exactly who she said she is. You can trust her."

"But how do you know that? You said yourself that she only tells you what you need to know."

"Makes it easier to do my job that way. Besides, I know Ava well. She's a woman of her word."

Tess still wasn't sure what exactly Riley's role was. They didn't act like a driver or a butler would. They had a casualness about them that seemed at odds with how an employee in such a formal role would behave.

"So, you know Ava well," Tess began. "Why does she live out here all by herself?"

"You'd have to ask her that," Riley replied.

Was Ava some kind of recluse? Did she live out here to shut herself away from everyone? Kidnapping aside, she didn't seem like the friendliest of people. Everything about her screamed 'stay away.'

So why was Tess still so drawn to her?

She changed the subject again. "So, Ava said I can have anything I want. I just need to ask you, right?"

Riley nodded. "I'll have to pass on any requests to Ava for approval, but she's made it clear that you're to have whatever you want."

Tess thought for a moment. "So if I wanted a pair of Jimmy Choos, I could have them?"

"Yes."

"First-edition copies of every Agatha Christie book?"

"If they could be found."

"A wide-screen TV?"

"If you wanted. But the house already has a theater with a state-of-the-art projector."

Riley didn't seem interested in entertaining Tess's childish questions any further. So they lapsed into silence as Tess headed up the grand staircase to the third floor. She was just about to turn down a hallway to the left when Riley stopped her with a firm hand on her shoulder.

"These are Ava's rooms. They're off limits."

"Right." Tess stepped back. "Sorry, I didn't realize."

But as she turned around, a door opened partway down the hall, Ava emerging from it.

She glanced at Tess before nodding to her driver. "Riley, can I speak to you?"

Riley gave Tess a firm look. "Stay there."

She remained planted in her place as Riley joined Ava, stepping through the door and shutting it behind them. Tess peered down the hallway. *So these are Ava's rooms.* The rooms she'd been told to stay out of.

Maybe Tess was feeling defiant. Maybe she was curious about the enigmatic woman who had captured her. But she wasn't going to stand around when she had the chance to sneak a look at Ava's rooms.

As quietly as she could, Tess crept down the hall, the old floorboards creaking beneath her feet. Most of the doors were closed, and when she tried the door handles, many were locked. But a couple were unlocked. One was a lounge room, with antique sofas and a long balcony, ivy curling around the railings.

The other unlocked room? It was even more interesting.

Tess poked her head through the door. Inside was a study, with bookshelves lining the walls and a large desk in the center of the room. And on the desk was a computer connected to a monitor.

I bet that has an internet connection. Just because Ava had forbidden Tess contact with the outside world, that didn't mean Ava herself didn't have access to it. Surely even someone as reclusive as her needed to use the internet now and then. And Tess had spotted a small satellite dish hidden at the back of the house earlier. It had stuck out to her because of how out of place it looked on the old building.

Sure enough, Tess spotted a small modem-like box blinking away on a cabinet by the desk.

Hmm...

Could she sneak inside and use the computer? Send someone a message? But who would she—

"What are you doing?" Ava's crisp voice sliced through the air. "I told you to stay out of my rooms."

Tess ducked her head back out the door, just in time to see Ava barreling toward her. She pulled the door shut, almost knocking Tess over, and locked it with a key she'd produced from her pocket.

Then, she fixed her dark gaze on Tess.

"I'm sorry!" Tess lowered her head. "I was just curious."

"I don't care. These rooms are off limits. *Do not* make me tell you again."

Tess nodded. "I won't."

"Now get out of my sight."

Tess hurried back down the hallway toward the staircase. It was only when she was safely in her bedroom, the door shut firmly behind her, that she was able to breathe again.

She collapsed onto the bed. Ava was *not* a woman she wanted to mess with. And she was not a woman Tess wanted to be trapped on an island with.

She couldn't trust Ava. She couldn't accept her fate. She needed to escape.

And her key to freedom was right in the middle of Ava's study.

Sure, the room was locked. But that was no problem for Tess. She could still get to that computer.

She would play along, fool Ava into thinking she was the perfect, obedient house guest. She would bide her time.

And when her moment came, she would seize it.

CHAPTER 7

Tess dove into the pool, starting her first of five laps.

Five laps. One for each day of being trapped in a mansion on an island. One for each day of being kept completely in the dark.

One for each day she'd spent waiting for her moment.

She was restless. She was scared. She had no one to turn to. Not Riley, who continued to follow her, watching her every move. And especially not Ava, a woman as mysterious as she was cold.

Ava was keeping her distance. Sure, they saw each other at mealtimes, but those were tense, formal affairs. Once, Tess had skipped dinner just to see what would happen, only to have Riley appear at her bedroom door with a tray of food, along with a strongly worded message from Ava that she expected Tess to come down for dinner every day to check in. Tess hadn't dared defy her orders since.

Because despite what Ava had said at breakfast that first morning, she *was* Ava's prisoner.

So why couldn't Tess stop thinking about her? Why was

Ava all she could see when she closed her eyes at night as she lay in bed, all alone? Why did Ava's very presence make her whole body burn?

Tess pushed the feeling down, focusing instead on her form as she flipped and kicked off the wall, starting her second lap. She'd never been a good swimmer, but she needed to do something with all her energy. And she needed to kill time until she could get into Ava's study to use her computer. She went to the gym every morning, running on the treadmill until she couldn't run anymore. She wandered the island, walking circles around it for miles and miles, until the sun set and Riley insisted she return to the house. She read an entire book from the mansion's library every single day.

And today, she was taking advantage of the pool, yet another diversion Ava had so generously provided her. Along with the bikini she was wearing, the fluffy white towels that were waiting for her by the pool for when she finished, the lavish lunch she'd eaten a couple of hours ago.

Ava was keeping her in a gilded cage. But a cage was still a cage.

Three laps. Four. Five. Until her arms burned and her muscles ached. She relished the sensation, the distraction it provided her troubled mind. But if she pushed herself any harder, she wouldn't be able to walk tomorrow.

She floated over to the edge of the pool and hoisted herself up out of the water. Riley was sitting on a chair nearby, the table beside them stacked with towels. Without a word to Riley, Tess grabbed a towel and began drying herself off. Riley barely acknowledged her either, which was just the way she liked it. At least this way she could pretend she didn't have a babysitter.

Wrapping the towel around her shoulders, she headed up to the deck off the side of the house. It was elevated over the grounds and led to a lounge room on the second floor. The sliding glass door leading into the house was locked, but she wasn't planning on going inside. She simply wanted some peace and privacy.

As she climbed the creaky stairs up to the deck, Riley didn't follow, seemingly content with watching her from afar. Tess made her way to the railing, admiring the view of the island and the sea beyond as she removed the towel from her shoulders, exposing them to the sun's rays. The day was warm enough for her to enjoy the sunshine on her skin before the afternoon chill settled in.

She leaned against the railing, taking it all in. Only a few seconds passed before she heard a sound behind her.

She turned. Ava stood behind the glass door, unlocking it with a key. Tess straightened up, her stomach filling with butterflies.

Ava opened the door and stepped out onto the deck carefully. "You shouldn't be out here."

"I'm sorry?" Did she mean the deck? Ava hadn't said anything about it being off limits before. And how had she known Tess was out here in the first place?

Had Ava been watching her?

Suddenly, Tess was very aware of how little she was wearing. Her bikini wasn't the skimpiest of the swimwear she'd found in her closet, but it wasn't exactly modest.

However, Ava wasn't looking at her body. She seemed to

be deliberately *not* looking, her intense gaze fixed on Tess's eyes. But it made her skin sizzle all the same.

Ava took a few steps toward her. "You shouldn't be out here," she repeated. "This deck is falling apart. It's unstable."

"Oh." Tess glanced at the surrounding deck. The wood looked to be rotting in places. She'd felt the planks creaking under her feet as she walked across the deck, but she hadn't thought anything of it. "I didn't know."

"You need to move, now. It's not safe." Ava stepped closer and held out her hand. "Come."

"Okay, let me—" Without thinking, Tess turned to grab her towel from where it was slung over the railing. But as she shifted her weight, the wood beneath her groaned.

It happened faster than she could blink. With a loud crack, the plank beneath her foot snapped, a jagged hole forming in its place. As her leg slipped through it, she managed to keep her balance. But before she could steady herself, the deck began to groan and creak again, the floor beneath her crumbling away.

Her stomach plummeted as she began to drop—

Suddenly, Ava's arms were around her, pulling her back onto solid ground. Holding onto Tess tightly, she dragged her to the safety of the solid wood by the door.

"I've got you," Ava said. "I've got you."

Tess's heart thumped wildly in her chest. Where she'd stood only seconds ago was now a gaping hole in the deck. How far down was the drop? Ten feet? More?

Don't think about that. She took a deep breath, trying to calm herself. But that only made her aware that she was in Ava's arms, their bodies pressed together. And for a woman so cold and hard, Ava was warm. Soft. Her skin. Her curves against Tess's bare skin. Her breath against Tess's face. And the scent of her, sweet and sharp like jasmine in the breeze.

Tess glanced up at her face. Ava looked back at her, that same fiery intensity in her eyes. But now, there was something else in them.

An unmistakable, unquenchable lust.

Ava exhaled softly. Her hold on Tess was unyielding, her lips barely an inch from Tess's own. Could she feel the electricity surging through Tess's body? Could she feel Tess quiver at her touch? Could she feel how Tess hungered for her, for those crimson lips, that velvet voice, beckoning her, *commanding* her—

Footsteps pounded on the stairs nearby. Tess turned. Riley was making their way up the stairs, swiftly but carefully, stopping before they reached the unstable wood of the deck.

"Are you okay?" Riley asked. "I saw what happened."

Tess nodded. At the same time, Ava seemed to remember herself. Ensuring Tess was on solid ground, Ava released her from her arms, ordering her into the safety of the house.

Tess obeyed, her heart still pounding. But it was just adrenaline. It had nothing to do with Ava. She didn't want Ava. How could she want a woman who was holding her captive?

No, what Tess wanted was her freedom. She couldn't lose sight of that. And she couldn't lose sight of her goal, which was hidden away in Ava's study.

She couldn't let her guard drop. No matter how enticing Ava was.

CHAPTER 8

"I owe you an apology."

"Hm?" Tess looked up from her plate. Her mind had been elsewhere.

Ava's delicate fingers tightened around even more delicate silverware. "I said, I owe you an apology. I should have warned you about the deck. That was my mistake."

"Er, it's fine." *How about an apology for dragging me here in the first place?* But Tess kept that thought to herself.

They lapsed into silence as they continued to eat. Dinner today was wine-braised short ribs, tender and rich, accompanied by a bottle of red wine with a name Tess couldn't pronounce. Tess rarely drank wine. It tasted like vinegar and made her mouth dry. But this wine was good. *Really* good. And so was the food, as usual. It was almost enough to make Tess forget the situation she was in.

From her seat at the head of the table, Ava took a small sip from her glass. "I see you went for a swim again today."

"Um, yes," Tess replied between bites. Had Riley told her that? Or had Ava been watching her, just like she had been

50

the day before when she'd saved Tess from the collapsing deck?

Heat rose to Tess's skin, the moment playing out in her mind. How she'd started to fall, only to be swept into Ava's arms. How Ava had held her close, so close that Tess could feel every curve of her body, her breath on her neck. She could almost feel it now, could almost taste Ava's lips—

Tess shoved the memory back into the depths of her mind. But that didn't stop her cheeks from burning.

Ava didn't seem to notice. "It's good to see you taking advantage of the amenities here."

The amenities. That made it sound like Tess was at some kind of luxury island resort.

Except she hadn't been given a choice to come to the resort.

And she couldn't leave.

And her jailer was a woman as frosty as she was alluring.

If things between her and Ava had been tense before, they'd only gotten worse after the incident on the deck. It was as if beneath Ava's icy demeanor were the faintest embers of desire, smoldering low but strong.

Or maybe Tess only wished there were.

Why did she feel that way toward Ava? It had to be desperation. Tess was lost, alone, afraid. In the face of mysterious forces plaguing her, Ava was the equally mysterious force who held Tess's safety in her hands.

She wanted answers. She wanted comfort. And Ava was the only person who could give her that, the only person who could reassure her that everything was all right. That was why Tess harbored such irrational, illogical feelings toward her.

Ava broke her out of her reverie. "I'd like to assure you that I'm working on resolving your... situation. But it's going to take some time. For now, do you have any requests? Things you need? Things you'd like to help pass the time?"

Tess shook her head. "No, I'm fine."

"Surely there's something you want. Perhaps not something you need, but something you desire?"

Ava's eyes locked with hers. Tess's lips parted, but no words came out. The way Ava was looking at her was intrusive and captivating at the same time. It was like she was stripping Tess bare, down to her very soul.

Ava leaned forward, her voice dropping low. "Tell me. What is it that you want?"

Tess's breath caught in her chest. Could Ava see her thoughts? Could she feel Tess's need?

Could she hear the way Tess's body whispered, *I want you*?

"I..." Tess blinked. What was wrong with her? She tore her eyes away, finding her voice again. "Nothing. There's nothing I want."

"If you say so." Ava sat back in her chair, picking up her knife and fork again. "I only ask because I'd like your stay here to be as comfortable as possible. So if there's anything you want, let me know and I'll make it happen."

"I will. Thank you." Tess set her cutlery down. "I'm finished. I'm going to my room."

Ava looked at Tess's plate with disapproval. "You've barely eaten anything."

"I'm not hungry."

She didn't wait to be dismissed before leaving the table.

She needed to escape Ava's gaze. And she needed to pull herself together.

Because if—*when*—her moment came, she couldn't miss it.

~

An hour later, Tess sat curled up in an armchair in the small living room next to her bedroom, reading a book from the mansion's library.

Mercifully, she was alone. Ava's driver and butler seemed to have many jobs, which occasionally meant leaving Tess unattended for short periods. But not long enough for Tess to get into any trouble.

This evening was one of those times. A flight carrying supplies from the mainland had arrived, and Riley had been tasked with bringing them back to the house.

But as Tess glanced out the window overlooking the front garden, it wasn't only Riley she spotted leaving the mansion and heading down to the airstrip.

Ava was with them.

Tess's heart leaped. Ava's rooms were unguarded. Riley wasn't around to stop Tess from going inside them.

This was the moment she'd been waiting for!

But she didn't have much time. Ava wouldn't leave her unattended for long. Making no attempt at stealth, Tess hurried to Ava's rooms. Sure, there was a chance she'd run into one of the few house staff, but it had never happened before. Were they deliberately staying out of Tess's way at Ava's orders? It seemed more likely they were instructed to be invisible, so the reclusive lady of the house didn't have to see or talk to anyone.

Tess reached the third floor and made a beeline for Ava's study. When she turned the door handle, it was locked.

But she'd expected that. And it was no obstacle to her. When she was in foster care, she'd been shipped from home to home. Many of those homes had been unpleasant, to say the least. She'd picked up some unusual habits just to survive.

Along with some unusual skills. And when the parents at one of her foster homes insisted on locking their foster children in their bedrooms every day from dusk till dawn to keep them out of trouble?

Tess had learned how to escape with nothing but a hairpin.

She pulled one from her hair. She'd already practiced on some of the other doors in the mansion when no one was looking. The old locks had been easy to pick.

Fortunately, the lock on Ava's door was no different. After less than a minute, Tess felt the telltale release of the lock.

Got it! She glanced back down the hall. There was no sign of Ava or anyone else. She opened the door and stepped carefully into the study. It was empty, just as she'd expected, the modem blinking away on the cabinet, the monitor on the desk black.

Tess rounded the desk and jiggled the mouse, waking up the screen. *Yes!* The computer was still logged in. Was Ava so used to living alone that she didn't think about locking her computer?

Tess wasn't going to question her luck. She took a seat in

the large leather desk chair and opened up a browser, logging into her messaging account. She had it all planned out. She would get a message to a friend asking them to send the police to come get her.

There was one problem with her plan. Tess didn't know where she was. All she could say was she'd been kidnapped by a strange woman and taken to an island in the middle of nowhere that wasn't on any maps. Even if someone believed her, what could they do with that information? How would they find her?

But it was the best plan she had. She needed to try.

Finally, the messaging app loaded. At once, she was flooded with a week's worth of messages, all from people asking her where she was. She didn't have any family or many friends, so they were mostly from her coworkers, who had grown worried when she hadn't shown up from work.

And there were several from Cherry herself, which started off mildly concerned, but slowly became angrier and angrier as time passed. Her latest message said that if Tess didn't turn up to work tomorrow, she wouldn't have a job any longer.

"Great, now I have to find another job." That was, if she ever got out of this mess.

But what had Ava said that night in the car? *Once this is over, none of that will matter.*

What did she mean?

The computer chimed as a new message came through. It was from Ashley.

"Hello? Tess? I can see you're online."

Right. She was supposed to be trying to contact someone to help her. Why not Ashley?

She began typing out a message urging Ashley to send help. But before she could finish it, a panicked reply appeared on the screen.

"Where the hell are you? I've been worried sick. And Cherry is so close to firing you. Are you okay? You never miss work. We all thought you'd died or something!"

"I'm fine," Tess reassured her. *"I haven't died, at least."*

"What does that mean? Are you in trouble?

Another message popped up on the screen.

"Is this about those guys who came looking for you?"

Tess's stomach dropped. She erased what she'd written. *"What guys? When?"*

"They came into the diner yesterday. There were two of them. Big guys dressed in black, ugly as hell. Looked like they could handle themselves."

Were those the men who had followed Tess home that night? It sure sounded like it.

"What did they want?" she sent.

"To know where you are. They asked everyone about you. Whether we'd heard from you, where we thought you'd gone, if you had any friends or relatives you might be staying with. They said they were with the police, but they weren't wearing uniforms. They didn't look like any cops I've ever seen. And Cherry seemed scared of them. It was really shady."

Tess's stomach dropped. Were those men connected to the police somehow? Were they cops themselves? Then why had they chased Tess down that night? Or had they only pretended to be cops to get her coworkers to talk?

Tess didn't know what to believe. But she was sure of

one thing. Ava had been right all along. Tess was in real danger. She couldn't risk trusting the police to keep her safe. She couldn't risk trusting Ashley not to tell those men where she was. And she couldn't put anyone else at risk by asking them to help her.

There was only one person left she could turn to. Ava. Her captor. Her protector. Whatever the hell Ava was.

But could Tess trust her?

"Well? Are you okay? Where are you? Say something!"

Tess took a deep breath and composed a reply. But she didn't get a chance to send it.

Because a moment later, the door to the study opened.

Tess froze in place. She had nowhere to hide. And it was already too late. Ava was looking straight at her.

Ava marched toward the desk and ripped the power cord out of the wall. The monitor on the table went black, the lights on the computer and modem going dark.

But Tess barely noticed. Because all her attention was fixed on Ava.

She loomed over Tess, white-hot fury in her eyes. *"What have you done?"*

Tess cringed into the chair. "I'm sorry! I just wanted to check my messages…"

"Did you speak to someone? Tell me!"

"Y-yes. My coworker. But that's all."

"What did you tell her?"

"I didn't tell her anything. Just that I'm okay."

"You expect me to believe that? That you broke into my office just to have a chat with your coworker?"

"Yes!" Tess hesitated. "Well, I was thinking of telling her the truth at first, but then she said some men went to the diner looking for me, and I realized things were serious, so I—"

Ava blanched. "What did you just say?"

"That some men went to the diner looking for me?"

"Yes, what men?"

"I don't know. There were two of them, big guys. They might have been the same guys from the other night, but they told everyone they were with the police. They questioned everyone at the diner about me. They wanted to know where I'd gone."

Ava turned to the door, a curse on her lips. "Get a message to Cassandra. Tell her I need to speak to her right away."

Only then did Tess notice Riley was standing in the doorway. They nodded, then disappeared down the hall.

"And *you*." Ava turned back to Tess, her gaze cold as frost. "You will go to your room, and you will stay there until I say you can leave. No more wandering the halls. No more having free roam of the island. Not when you keep defying me and putting your life at risk!"

"But—"

"Go. *Now.*"

Tess scrambled out of the chair and ran down the hallway, hot tears spilling from her eyes. She'd messed up. She'd lost her one lifeline to the outside world. The only person left who could help her was Ava.

And she'd just shattered any trust Ava had in her.

CHAPTER 9

A va packed the last of her clothes into the small suitcase. It was late at night, and she was leaving for an overnight trip to the mainland the next day.

She had important business to take care of. There was her job, to start. She'd made a career as a venture capitalist, investing in startups and small businesses. While she did most of her work from her home, she occasionally needed to meet with potential investees in person. She had one such meeting in the afternoon.

However, the most important event on her schedule tomorrow was finding out who was after Tess.

In the time since she'd brought Tess to the mansion, Ava had performed her own investigations, speaking to several lawyers and reaching out to the private investigator who helped her find Tess in the first place. But he'd been unable to dig up anything new.

There was only one person left who could help her. And that was the very person who had recommended the PI to Ava in the first place—Cassandra Lee. She was arguably the most powerful woman on the whole continent, a fact very few people were aware of.

But Cassandra refused to do business remotely, which meant Ava had no choice but to pay her a visit. She'd been planning to do so soon enough, however, the incident in the study had made meeting with Cassandra a matter of urgency.

I can't believe Tess did that. It had been partially Ava's fault for leaving her computer unattended. But she couldn't have predicted that Tess would get into her locked study. Because it *had* been locked. Ava was certain of it.

Was Tess so desperate to get away from her that she'd resorted to breaking into her locked office? Could Ava blame her? Other than saving her life, she'd given Tess little reason to trust her.

If Tess had any sense, she wouldn't trust me. I've already failed her.

Ava placed her carefully packed toiletries bag on top of the silk nightgown in her suitcase. *Stop wallowing in your guilt.* She'd made that promise years ago. But a promise was a promise. And Ava hadn't kept hers.

A fact she was reminded of every time Tess looked at her with expectant eyes. They always seemed to plead something of Ava. Not just for the answers Tess so clearly wanted, and deserved. No, what Ava saw in her eyes was a longing that made Ava's heart race, made her yearn to possess her in every way a woman could.

But that evening in her study, all Ava had seen in Tess's eyes was hurt. It was a natural reaction to Ava's anger. But her anger was born of fear, fear for Tess's life. By contacting the outside world, Tess had risked her safety. She'd put her life in danger all over again.

But Ava had checked Tess's browser history after banishing her to her room. She'd read Tess's messages. She'd seen for herself that Tess was telling the truth. She hadn't told anyone anything.

Was she beginning to trust Ava after all?

There was a knock on her bedroom door. Ava had left it open, which Riley took as an invitation to stroll right into the room.

"Heading to the mainland?" they asked.

"First thing in the morning," Ava replied. "I'll likely stay overnight, so I'll need you to keep an eye on Tess for me."

"To keep anyone from getting to her, or to make sure she doesn't try anything?"

Ava zipped her suitcase shut. "Both." Had she been overly cautious in having Riley follow Tess everywhere? Perhaps. But the other night in the study had proved it necessary.

Riley folded their arms across their chest. "I wasn't hired to be a babysitter."

"I know. And I appreciate that you've taken this job despite it being outside of your usual skill set. I need someone I can trust."

"You can always count on me. And, I don't normally like to stick my nose into these things, but…"

Ava sighed. "Just spit it out."

"It's about Tess. Don't you think you're being a little too hard on her?"

"No, I don't. She's proven she's unable to follow my

rules. And she compromised her safety without even realizing it."

"It's only natural that she's reacting this way. You took her away from her life, cut her off from the world, and are keeping her locked up in a mansion in the middle of nowhere without even telling her why. What did you expect?"

"I let her out of her room, didn't I?" The morning after the incident in the study, Ava had told Riley to allow Tess free roam of the mansion again. But only during daylight hours. And only with Riley present. "It's for her own good."

"Is ignoring her for her own good too? You haven't said a word to her in days."

Ava pressed her lips together. From the outside, it looked like she was ignoring Tess to punish her for breaking into her study. In reality, Ava simply didn't want to face the maelstrom of conflicting feelings Tess brought about in her. Feelings she refused to indulge.

"Even before the night in your study, you were acting cold toward her," Riley said. "If you want her to listen to you —*trust* you—you need to stop treating her like garbage."

"I am *not* treating her like garbage."

But Riley was right. If Ava wanted Tess's trust, she would need to give her *something*.

"All right," she said. "Tess can have free run of the house *without* you following her. But I still expect you to keep an eye on her."

Riley raised an eyebrow. "You're going to have to do better than that."

"*Fine*. And I'll apologize to her for yelling at her the other night."

"That's a start. At the very least, it should defuse some of the tension between you. Seriously, it's making the atmosphere in the house unbearable."

Was the tension between them that noticeable?

What else had Riley noticed between Ava and Tess?

"Anyway, I'm turning in for the night," they said, heading for the door. "And just so you know, Tess is still awake if you want to talk to her before you leave."

Ava dismissed Riley and set her suitcase aside. She would apologize, but nothing more. She couldn't let Tess get too close. Because every time Ava was around her, she felt the unmistakable pull of attraction. *Mutual* attraction.

And it would be so easy to give in to temptation…

But Ava could never, *ever* go there with her. Tess was off limits in so many ways. She represented everything Ava had ever desired.

And that was dangerous.

She knocked on Tess's bedroom door. "It's Ava." When she didn't get an answer, she said, "I'm coming in."

She waited a few moments before opening the door. The room was dark, save for a lamp in the corner. Beside it, Tess sat on a chaise lounge, a blanket over her legs and knees pulled up underneath her chin. A pile of books sat on the floor beside her, untouched. Instead, Tess was staring across the room at nothing at all.

As Ava approached, Tess glanced briefly in her direction before hugging her knees even tighter to her chest.

Ava stopped a few feet away from her. *Don't get too close.*

But Tess didn't seem to want her to get close either. The way she avoided Ava's gaze said as much.

Ava cleared her throat, breaking the silence between them. Tess finally looked up at her. Like always, her eyes seemed to plead with Ava…

Stop. She needed to focus. She needed to do what she came here to do, and only that.

"I'm sorry," she said.

Tess blinked. "Oh. Okay."

"I mean it. I'm sorry for being so harsh with you the other night, and ever since. It was wrong of me."

"It's all right. You were just looking out for me. I understand that now. I didn't at first, but I've had a lot of time to think about it. And I was telling the truth when I said I didn't talk to anyone except my coworker. I swear I didn't tell her anything."

"I know. And I'm not angry with you. While I was angry with you for sneaking around and breaking into my study, I was more concerned about your safety. But I understand why you did it, given the situation you're in. All this time, I've expected you to trust me when I've given you no reason to."

Tess shook her head. "That's just it. It's the silliest thing. You're a stranger. You practically abducted me off the street. I shouldn't trust you. So why does a part of me feel like I *should* trust you?"

"You should. I've said from the beginning that I won't let any harm come to you, Tess. I mean it."

Her gaze shifted out into the distance. "It's just so hard to know what to believe, what to feel. This is all just crazy. A week ago, my life was so mundane. All I did was work every shift I could just to try to get ahead a little. But it was never enough. Not enough to escape the cycle of work and bills, work and bills. Not to escape how miserable I was. Because I have nothing. No family. No relationships. No career. Nothing."

Guilt gnawed in Ava's mind. She'd had the power to give Tess a better life all along, but she hadn't done a thing.

"Then suddenly, my life is upended by these men who show up out of nowhere, who want to hurt me?" Tess's voice quivered. "I try not to let myself feel it. It's what I've always done, ever since I was a kid, because how else do you cope with that? But I've been afraid to sleep at night, because when I lie there in bed, everything I've been trying not to think about, trying not to feel, comes flooding back…"

She looked up at Ava, eyes shimmering with tears. Something tightened in Ava's chest.

"I'm so scared," Tess said softly. "When I let myself stop and think about it, it paralyzes me. I had nothing, and now I've even lost that. And I could have lost my *life*. I know I didn't imagine that gun. I know it."

Tess closed her eyes and took a deep breath. But it barely calmed her.

"I'd give anything just to go back to how things used to be," she said. "To my miserable, empty life. To my shitty job, to Cherry trying to steal my tips. To my run-down apartment, where I spent every night cold and alone. Because that's what my life has always been. I'm used to it. And it's so much better than being lost and scared like I am now."

Tears spilled onto Tess's cheeks. Ava felt a pang of sympathy. *Don't get close.*

Yet before she could stop herself, she was sitting next to Tess on the chaise.

"I'm sorry," she said. "For all of this. For ripping you away from your life. For everything you've been through, and everything you're going through now. But believe me when I say that you *will* get through this. And when it's all over, your life will be better. You won't have to worry about anything ever again."

Tess looked into her eyes. "You've said that before, but what does it mean? What's going to happen when all this is over?"

For a moment, Ava's iron resolve wavered. How could she sit here, just inches from the young woman whose every desire she longed to make reality, whose every wish she longed to grant, and deny her the truth? How could she sit here and look into those anguished eyes when she had the power to make all of Tess's pain go away?

How could she sit here and not draw Tess into an embrace, whispering all the thoughts, sweet and sinful, that filled her mind every time she gazed upon the woman she craved with an intensity that set her ablaze?

But all she did was set a reassuring hand on Tess's arm. "I can't tell you that. Not yet. But when the time is right, I will. I need you to trust me on that. And I need you to trust me to keep you safe."

Tess slid her feet down to the floor, the blanket slipping from her legs. She was dressed only in an oversized sleep shirt that barely covered her thighs. But Ava resisted the temptation to look.

"I don't know whether I trust you or not. But I..." Tess

glanced down at her lap, then peered up at Ava from under her eyelashes. "I feel safe with you. I do."

Ava set her hand on top of Tess's. At that moment, Tess was all she could see. Tess, the woman she'd searched for so long. Tess, the woman who stirred every wicked impulse within her.

Tess, the woman she wanted with an intensity she hadn't felt since she was a teenager first learning what it meant to *want*.

She was right here, in Ava's grasp. All Ava had to do was claim her.

But before she could move or speak, Tess's lips were on hers, first soft and slow, then hungry, pleading. Ava deepened the kiss, a fire raging through her body as she devoured Tess's lips, breathed in her sweet scent, savored her desire.

It was intoxicating. Ava was drunk on it, drunk on her, losing herself, losing control—

She tore herself away, rising to her feet. Tess gazed up at her, confusion in her eyes, her cheeks still wet with tears.

Ava shook her head. "That was a mistake."

Tess winced. "Why? Ava, I—"

"No. This cannot happen again."

Ava turned on her heel and marched to the door. As she opened it wide, she caught a glimpse of Tess on the chaise, her knees drawn up to her chin, hugging her legs to her body again.

Ava steeled herself. "Goodnight, Tess."

It took all her willpower to step through the door and shut it behind her.

CHAPTER 10

S *top thinking about Tess.*

And yet, as Ava sat in the back seat of the car ferrying her from the airfield into the city, thoughts of Tess continued to plague her.

From the moment they met, Ava had been tempted. But she'd resolved to resist her urges, resolved to not give in.

But it had been Tess who kissed *her*.

Why? Why had Tess kissed her, despite Ava's best attempts at keeping her at arm's length? Why had Tess kissed her, a stranger who had stormed into her life only to take her away from it with no explanation?

Could Tess feel the thread of fate that bound them together, even if she didn't know what it was?

But that thread was the reason Ava couldn't touch her. It was one of many reasons, but it was the most important of them all.

Ava was almost forty. She was far too old to let lust control her. She lived a life defined by self-discipline, by order. She could master her carnal desires.

Because that was all her feelings for Tess were. Pure physical attraction, combined with a drive to protect her.

The car pulled up to her destination. It was an old sandstone building in the middle of the city, standing proud in a sea of skyscrapers that jutted up into the air. It was certainly a fitting home for the Queens Club. While Cassandra Lee, the club's founder and owner, wasn't known for her sense of humor, Ava wouldn't put it past the woman to have chosen the building for that exact reason.

Ava stepped out onto the sidewalk, taking a moment to appreciate the building and all that it stood for. The Queens Club was—as Cassandra liked to put it in her more blunt moments—a 'fuck you' to the gentlemen's clubs of old. It was a way for powerful women to find like-minded people and get a leg up in the patriarchal, sexist, nepotistic world.

Ava entered the building and nodded to the woman at the door, who knew all the club's members by sight. While club membership was exclusive, it wasn't based on wealth. Instead, it was based on success and influence. From businesswomen and politicians to celebrities and even scientists —any woman who was anyone on the entire North American continent was a member of the club. And its members were the only people who knew the club existed.

Ava strode through the hallways, only crossing paths with a few other people. At this time of the morning, the club was almost empty, a handful of members and staff scattered around. The club served as a valuable private space for networking and socializing, and it was equipped with all the amenities needed to facilitate its purpose. It sported a fully serviced dining room, a bar, a poolroom. There were suites members could stay in, and a range of recreational facilities, including a gym, a sauna, and a pool.

But Ava wasn't here to make use of the amenities. She was here to see Cassandra.

She was the person who ran it all. She had more power and connections than any other woman on the continent. And although very few people knew it, not all those connections were aboveboard. Which was exactly why Ava had come to see her.

Her connections in both high and low places were part of the reason Cassandra only did business in person. It didn't leave a paper trail. But on top of that, keeping Queens Club business on location was a rule for all members. It was a way to encourage the kind of in-person networking that fostered connections. That was the entire purpose of the Queens Club.

Ava rode the elevator up to the top floor and made her way to Cassandra's office. The door was open in anticipation of Ava's arrival. As she stepped through it, Cassandra looked up from her seat behind her large teak desk. Her long black hair was pulled back in a tight bun, her dark eyes keen as ever.

She gave a nod of greeting. "Ava."

Ava took a seat in front of desk. "Good to see you."

That was the friendliest the two of them ever got. But despite appearances, she and Cassandra were close. They understood each other, understood that they both carried ghosts from their pasts. And they both understood not to ask each other questions about them. Ava suspected that Cassandra's ghosts were far worse than her own.

But she was one of the few people in the world Ava

trusted. They met in business school and had been friends ever since. And Cassandra was a good friend to have. Behind her stone veneer was a keen intellect that could cut through any obstacle. She used it in her day job as CEO of her investment firm. And she used it to run the Queens Club.

She shut her laptop and placed it to the side. "You said you have something urgent to discuss. Is this about Tess?"

"Yes." Cassandra was the reason Ava had found Tess in the first place. After trying to find her through conventional means, including several private investigators, Ava had asked for Cassandra's help. Cassandra had referred her to her own personal PI, who did the kind of work that wasn't strictly legal. But he was effective. And after months of searching, Ava finally found Tess, alive and well.

Now, Ava had to keep her that way.

"So you've found her," Cassandra said.

"I have. Unfortunately, I wasn't the only one. She was pursued by a pair of armed men on her way home from work just over a week ago. I was forced to take action. I have her somewhere safe, but those men are still after her. They returned to the diner, posing as police so they could question her coworkers about where she went. I need to know why. I need to know who sent them."

"They were armed, you say? Professionals?"

"I believe so. I'm no expert, but they didn't look like street-level thugs. Riley agrees. And I already spoke to your PI, but he couldn't find anything on them."

"That's not surprising. True professionals are beyond even his purview."

"But not yours?" Ava asked.

"Not mine. I'll look into it, see if my contacts have heard anything." Cassandra paused. "The men. What do you think they wanted with her?"

"It's hard to know for sure. They could have been sent to find out what Tess knows, or to rough her up as a way of intimidating her. Or they could have been sent to take her off the playing field altogether."

"I'm guessing you already have some ideas about who sent the men?"

"It could only be the Holdens. All of this coincided with Marcus's death." The billionaire heir had been driving recklessly and crashed his Ferrari into a tree. He'd remained on life support for a week before his family pulled the plug. "It has to be someone who's trying to protect their claim to his wealth. His wife is the most likely culprit. Or his parents. They all have enough money to hire professionals like those who attacked Tess."

Cassandra nodded. "I'll look into them. See what I can dig up. And I'll ask around, see if I can find out who those men were and who hired them."

Ava didn't question how exactly Cassandra was going to do that. While the woman rarely spoke of her past, Ava had picked up enough to know that Cassandra's image as an upright businesswoman and CEO hid a far more checkered background.

Ava reached into her purse. "I have something for you." She pulled out a small ziplock bag containing a swab inside a tube and placed it carefully on the desk. "For the DNA test."

It had been easy enough to get a sample of Tess's DNA from a glass she'd used. Not that Ava needed it. She already knew she had the right girl. But she needed to be sure. Especially if she was going to tell Tess everything.

Cassandra took the bag and slipped it into the top drawer of the desk. "I'll have the results for you in a week or two." She leaned back in her chair, studying Ava intently. "How are you doing? This business with Tess is getting messy. It can't be easy."

How much had Cassandra figured out? Ava had only told her what she needed to know. She and Riley were the only other people who had any idea of Tess's identity, and even then, they didn't know the whole truth. Fortunately, Riley had never been the type to ask questions, which was exactly why Ava had trusted them to help protect Tess.

Cassandra was the same. The woman had plenty of secrets of her own, after all. But now, even she was asking questions.

"I'm fine. But I can't deny that I'll be glad when this is all over." Ava leaned back, crossing her legs. "Now, I believe you had some club business you wanted to discuss with me?"

"I simply wanted your thoughts on some potential members. But it can wait until we're finished."

"The Queens Club can always use more members. Who are the candidates?"

"Stop trying to change the subject. I'll give you their files to take a look at once we're done talking about Tess."

"As far as I'm concerned, we *are* done," Ava said firmly.

"Perhaps you are. But I'm not. You know I'm not one to pry. And your business is your own. But your obsession with this girl has gotten you tangled up with some dangerous people."

"Oh, I'm aware."

"Then why are you doing this? I don't understand it. Why is Tess so important to you?"

Why *did* Ava care about what happened to Tess? The girl wasn't her responsibility. And when she'd made that promise years ago, she hadn't been in a position to fulfill it.

But a promise was a promise.

"Who is she to you?" Cassandra asked. "Really?"

Ava chose her words carefully. "She's someone I vowed to protect."

That was all Tess was to her. And it was all she could ever be.

No matter how much Ava wanted her.

CHAPTER 11

Tess paced her bedroom, even more restless and confused than before. *What the hell was I thinking, kissing her like that?*

But she *hadn't* been thinking. It had just happened. She'd been so consumed by all she was feeling that desire had taken over, possessing her body to act on its own.

But that didn't mean Tess hadn't wanted it.

She collapsed onto the bed with a sigh. It didn't matter what she wanted. Ava had rejected her. And then she'd disappeared for almost two whole days.

Was the timing a coincidence? All Riley would tell her was that Ava had gone to the mainland. Had she felt the need to get as far away from Tess as possible? Had the kiss repelled her that much?

Or had it been the opposite?

Because Ava's rejection of her hadn't been immediate. Tess had felt it when she kissed her. She felt how much Ava wanted her. She felt the woman's relentless hunger, tasted the need on her lips. Only for a moment, but it had been there.

Was that what Tess had sensed in her this entire time? Was that what she felt in Ava's piercing gaze, in her coldness, the distance she kept between them? Was she constantly holding herself back?

"This cannot happen again." What was the meaning behind those words? What was Ava hiding beneath her stone facade? Why, every time Tess looked at her, did she see a woman struggling to restrain herself?

Of course, Tess could have been wrong. Maybe Ava's rejection of her was just that. Because why would Ava want *her*? It was crazy that she wanted Ava in the first place. Ava, her captor. Ava, her protector. Ava, her savior. All of those things rolled into one.

Lines were blurring. Boundaries dissolving. Tess's control over her life slipping away. She needed something to ground her, something to hold on to. She needed—

Ava?

Yes, that was her voice in the hallway, along with Riley's. She was back from the mainland.

And she was heading toward Tess's room.

Her stomach flipped. How could she face Ava when she was such a mess?

But she didn't have a chance to gather herself before there was a knock on the door.

"Tess?" Ava said. "Can I come in?"

"One minute!" She grabbed the light robe hanging from her bedpost and wrapped it around herself, providing a little extra coverage on top of her thin nightshirt.

Then she hurried to the door, opening it wide to come face to face with Ava.

Ava stepped into the room, Riley following behind her. The driver carried several parcels wrapped in brown paper, which they set on a table to the side. With a nod to Ava, they left the room, leaving Tess and Ava alone.

She stood before Ava, barely able to meet her eyes. But that only left Tess looking at other parts of her. Her lithe legs, bare and toned in her heels. Her hips, made even more enticing by the fitted black dress she wore. Her lips, a shade of scarlet that surely matched Tess's cheeks right now.

Ava gestured toward the parcels stacked on the table. "These are for you. Some things I picked up to help you feel more comfortable."

Tess searched Ava's face, but couldn't read anything on it. Was this her way of extending an olive branch?

Or was it something else?

"It's clothing," Ava continued. "I took note of the clothes you favor and got you some more along those lines. And some books. Mysteries. At the rate you've been reading through the mysteries in the library, you'll soon need more."

Tess glanced between Ava and the packages. "You got all this for me? Why?"

"As I've said, I want you to be comfortable."

"So this has nothing to do with the other night?"

Ava tensed. "The other night was—"

"What? A mistake? Because I don't think it was."

Tess's pulse quickened. Did she dare speak the thoughts coalescing in her mind? Did she dare poke the beast that guarded her cage?

It was stupid. Dangerous. But everything she felt for Ava

—all the lust and desire, all the fear and confusion—was rising to a boiling point.

She couldn't keep it in any longer.

"You know what I think?" she said. "I think you feel something for me. Something you think you shouldn't feel. So you're doing all this—spoiling me, showering me with gifts, trying to keep me 'comfortable'—because it's the only way you'll let yourself indulge those feelings."

Something flickered behind Ava's eyes. Surprise, followed by resignation.

Tess was right.

And she wasn't finished. "You *want* me. But you won't let yourself have me. So you keep me here in this cage and give me all these nice things like I'm your pet because it's the closest you can get."

Ava's whole body stiffened. "That's not—"

"You don't have to deny it. Because I want you too." Tess stepped toward her. "I kissed you, Ava. *I* kissed *you*. And I felt you. I felt how much you—"

"Fine!" Ava's dark eyes locked on Tess. "You're right. I want you. I've wanted you from the moment we met."

Tess's breath caught in her chest. Hearing those words from Ava's lips was almost as thrilling as kissing her had been.

"But I've been keeping my distance," Ava said. "Because nothing can ever happen between us."

Tess bit back a groan. "Why do you keep saying that? I don't understand. Is it because you're older than me?"

"That's one reason."

"That doesn't bother me. I wouldn't have kissed you if it did. I wouldn't have kissed you if I didn't want this."

"It doesn't matter what you want, *or* what I want. I can't get close to you."

"Why? Can't you just tell me why?"

Tess waited silently. And when Ava finally spoke, it was with a whispered growl that sent shivers spreading along Tess's skin.

"Because if I do, I won't be able to hold myself back."

Tess's heart hammered against the inside of her chest. "You don't need to. Whatever it is that's making you feel like you have to stay away from me, I don't care. I want this."

She looked up into Ava's eyes. The resolve in them was crumbling to dust.

And in its place, desire blazed hot and bright.

Tess inhaled a deep breath, fortifying herself against Ava's intense gaze. Slowly, she slipped her robe from her shoulders, revealing the thin, short nightshirt she wore underneath.

"Please," she whispered. "Don't hold back."

Her words turned into a gasp as Ava's lips crashed against hers in a blistering kiss that nearly knocked her off her feet. But Ava's arms were around her, steadying her, pulling her close. Tess dissolved into Ava's body, losing herself in her. In the taste of her lips, the jasmine scent of her hair, the softness of her curves and the firmness of her hold.

As she lowered Tess onto the bed, Ava's grip didn't falter. Neither did the fire on her lips, the press of her body. Demanding hands slid down Tess's sides, tearing at the edges of her nightshirt, caressing the curves of her hips and waist, the mounds of her breasts. Her fingertips glided over Tess's nipples through the thin fabric of her nightshirt, stroking and circling until they turned into tiny, hard peaks.

Tess clutched blindly at Ava, seeking something to hold on to, seeking to spur her on. But there was no controlling the tempest that was Ava. She ripped Tess's nightshirt over her head, tearing two of the buttons, and tossed it aside to gaze down at Tess's body ravenously.

Heat rose to her skin. She still had her panties on, but she felt more naked than she ever had before. Here she was, in a secluded mansion on a remote island, the captive of a stranger who had complete control over her. Over what she did, where she went. Who she talked to, what she wore. Ava held Tess's very life in her hands. She was at Ava's mercy.

So why did that make Tess burn so hot? Why did that make her want Ava *more*?

Why did something so dangerously twisted feel so good?

Her hands trembled as she reached for the woman on top of her, wanting to draw her closer. Without warning, Ava grabbed onto Tess's wrists, pinning them effortlessly to the pillow above her head.

A pleasured gasp flew from Tess's lips. Ava smothered it with a kiss, tender but unyielding, until all Tess could do was shudder and moan.

She sank into the bed, giving in to Ava's sweet dominance. Hadn't Tess dreamed of this before? Of being taken like this, becoming a woman's possession? While other girls fantasized about the kind of lovemaking that was passionate and gentle, she'd always craved something more. She wanted to be consumed by her lover, mastered by her, *claimed* by her.

But she'd never shared her twisted fantasies with anyone. Not until now.

"Ava," she whispered. "I'm yours."

Ava's grip tightened around Tess's wrists. "Don't speak. Not unless you're begging me."

But she didn't give Tess a chance to beg before assailing every inch of her with scorching hands and searing kisses. She slid her fingertips over Tess's breasts, branding them with her lips and tongue. She drew her hands down Tess's hips and thighs, exploring parts of her rarely touched. She teased Tess through her now wet panties with relentless fingers until Tess ached with anticipation.

"Please," she whimpered. "Please!"

Ava's breath grew heavy. She took the waistband of Tess's panties and tore them down her legs. Then, Ava's fingers were inside her, filling her completely.

She cried out, her eyes squeezing shut and her head falling back. Ava was unhesitating in her thrusts, delving and plunging, stroking that sweet spot inside. At the same time, her lips and fingers roamed Tess's body, sending tremors and gasps through her.

"Yes," Ava purred. "I want to feel you unravel around my fingers. I want to hear you praise my name."

Tess arched against her, whispering her name over and over. *Ava. Ava. Ava.* A mantra. A prayer. At that moment, she was Tess's whole world.

As she succumbed to Ava and the pleasure she bestowed upon her possession, the woman's deep, velvet voice broke through Tess's fevered haze.

"Come for me."

Not a heartbeat later, an eruption went off deep inside

Tess's core. A wordless cry rose from her as she convulsed against Ava, who was pressed against her firmly as if to receive the full force of the pleasure rippling through her body. It was almost too much for Tess. But Ava rode it out with her until they crashed back down to earth.

It wasn't until the aftershocks subsided that Ava withdrew, pulling Tess into a fiery, possessive kiss. Tess relished Ava's strength, her control, her mastery over Tess's body and desires.

Ava had awoken something in her, that part of her that craved this, *needed* this. And as she held Tess in her arms, shielding her from all that troubled her, Tess could sense that something had awoken in Ava too. A lioness, commanding, protective, *hungry*.

And Tess wanted to feel her roar.

CHAPTER 12

W*hat have I done?*
That single thought echoed through Ava's mind as she lay in bed, embracing Tess as she dozed. Here she was, safe in Ava's grasp. The woman she'd been searching for. The woman she swore to protect.

The woman who was entirely forbidden to her.

This was wrong. So why didn't it *feel* wrong?

One thing was certain. Her feelings for Tess went beyond physical lust. However, that didn't make them real. She and Tess were connected, their lives inextricably intertwined. Ava felt the pull of their connection every time they were together.

But how much of that pull was because of their shared past, because of Ava's vow?

She needed to get away so she could separate her irrational feelings from her rational thoughts. It was impossible to think straight with Tess in her arms, sleeping like an angel. But it would be wrong to disturb her—

No. Taking care not to wake her up, Ava unraveled her

arms from around Tess's body and got up slowly from the bed.

She was halfway to the door when Tess spoke.

"Don't go. Not yet."

Ava froze in place. Why was it so hard to resist that voice? Why was it so hard to say no to her?

"Stay. *Please*, Ava."

Please. That one little word bored straight into Ava's heart, overshadowing all her doubts.

"All right," she said. "I'll stay."

"For the whole night?"

Ava nodded. "The whole night."

She slipped back into the bed, joining Tess under the covers. Tess snuggled against her chest, a grateful smile on her lips.

"Thank you," she whispered. "I needed this. I don't mean the sex. Well, not *just* the sex."

A pink flush blossomed on Tess's cheeks.

"What is it?" Ava asked.

"I guess I needed the way it made me feel. Reassured. Like everything is under control. And you gave me that. You *took* control and made me feel like you wouldn't let go of it, no matter what I did. I... I liked that."

Desire sparked inside Ava, along with hesitation. So Tess had sensed that in her? She hadn't intended to let Tess see that side of her. She'd been so caught up in the moment.

"But I could tell you were holding back." Tess peered up at her from under hooded eyes. "You don't need to hold yourself back from me. When I say I want you, I mean it. I want the *real* you. I want to feel what it's like when you really let go."

Something stirred in the depths of Ava's being. She silenced it. Tess didn't know what she was asking. She didn't understand. No one had ever understood that side of Ava. Not past lovers, flings. No one.

She shook her head. "You don't want that."

"How would you know?" Tess said.

"My tastes, they're not for the faint of heart."

"You think that describes me? You think I'm some fragile little thing that you're going to break? Because I'm far tougher than I look, Ava. Life hasn't exactly been sunshine and roses for me."

"I know. That's not what I meant." Ava rolled onto her back, her gaze wandering up to the ceiling. "It's not about you. It's about me."

For a moment, there was only silence.

Then, Tess reached out and drew a tentative hand up the center of Ava's chest. "What is it that you want when you look at me? I can see it in your eyes. There's something more there, something you long for. Show me."

Ava shook her head. "You're too inexperienced." Tess's bashful eagerness made that obvious.

"Then teach me," she pleaded.

Christ. This woman will be the death of me. "You don't know what you're asking of me."

"Maybe I do. Maybe I don't. But I want to find out. And didn't you say I should trust you? I'm trusting you with this."

"Perhaps you shouldn't trust me after all," Ava murmured.

"Why not?"

Because Ava had already betrayed her trust by keeping a

lifetime of secrets from her. And when she found out the truth, Tess wouldn't be able to look at her the same way.

Then end this. End this now.

But as Ava looked back into Tess's eyes, she just couldn't do it. She couldn't hurt her.

No, that was a lie. She was simply being selfish. Ava didn't want to lose her.

"I know you carry some kind of pain inside you," Tess said softly. "I don't know what it is, but I can see it." She traced her fingers down Ava's cheek. "Whatever it is? Whatever you think it makes you? It doesn't matter to me."

Why did Tess believe that, despite everything? Despite Ava dragging her off to an island and locking her up? Despite Ava treating her so coldly? Her heart was too pure, her soul too trusting.

Which was why Ava owed her the truth. She'd have to tell her sooner or later.

Ava only prayed it wouldn't destroy her.

CHAPTER 13

W hen Tess awoke the next morning, she found the bed next to her empty, the rumpled sheets illuminated by the sliver of sunlight slipping between a gap in the curtains. Had Ava left during the night after promising to stay?

But as Tess sat up and rubbed her eyes, she caught a glimpse of the clock on the nightstand. It was 11 a.m. She'd slept in.

She yawned and stretched. She hadn't had a good night's sleep in years, let alone since arriving at the mansion. She'd spent every night on the island tossing and turning, her short bouts of sleep plagued by fitful dreams and nightmares.

But last night? For the first time in a long time, she'd fallen asleep feeling safe. Secure. And she'd slept for twelve hours straight.

No wonder Ava had left. Tess didn't expect her to stick around for that long. She was surprised Ava had agreed to stay the night at all.

She was even more surprised they'd had sex in the first place.

Had it just been a dream? No, the scent of Ava's hair was still on the pillow beside her. And she could remember it all so vividly. The taste of Ava's skin on her lips. The feeling of Ava inside her, somehow gentle and unyielding at the same time.

Tess longed to feel it all again. She longed to see that part of Ava that she'd caught a glimpse of, the part that had awakened. She longed to see the woman Ava was when she really let go.

Not of control, but of her inhibitions. Because Ava was all about control. She wanted to lose herself in the absolute power she wielded over her prize.

And that was exactly what Tess wanted of her. That was what she craved. To feel the full force of Ava's desire. To be Ava's prize.

What did it say about Tess that she wanted this from a woman who had her trapped and isolated, completely under her control? But it wasn't like these twisted desires were new to her. She'd never dared to voice them, never had them fulfilled. But Ava brought them to the surface and made them impossible to ignore.

Which was why she wanted Ava so badly. Her heart fluttered as she replayed that moment in her mind, the moment Ava had held her down right here on the bed and kissed her until all her troubles melted away. In that moment, she had been nothing more than Ava's possession.

And it had been wonderful.

How she yearned to be Ava's for more than just a night…

But that was a crazy thought. Tess barely knew the

woman. And Ava was still keeping all these secrets from her, keeping her in the dark. Not to mention keeping her captive.

Because despite everything, Tess had no doubt that if she marched up to Ava and demanded to be taken home, Ava would say *no*.

She got out of bed and headed into her ensuite. After a quick shower, she left her bedroom and went downstairs in search of food to quiet her growling stomach. She was pleasantly surprised to find a tray with a selection of her favorite breakfast foods waiting for her in the dining room. Had the invisible kitchen staff taken note of what she usually ate? Or had Ava done so herself, as she had with the clothing Tess wore and the books she read?

But she had far more important things to do than ponder that question. She devoured her breakfast, then took off in search of Ava. Tess needed to talk to her, needed assurance that what had happened the night before had been real, had been meaningful. She needed to know that Ava wouldn't dismiss it as a mistake, just like the kiss.

But Ava wasn't in any of her usual spots in the common areas. And her rooms were off limits to Tess. Did she dare knock on Ava's door? Despite what had happened between them, she didn't want to break any of Ava's rules.

No, even more so after what had happened between them. Now, she understood that Ava was a woman who took her personal boundaries seriously.

But before Tess could decide what to do, she ran head-first into Riley. Literally, because she'd been distracted by thoughts of Ava.

"Sorry!" She took a step back. "I was looking for Ava. Do

you know where she is?"

"She went for a walk around the island," Riley replied.

Tess deflated. The island was huge. How was she supposed to find Ava if she was off wandering around it? "Okay. Thanks."

As Tess turned to leave, Riley spoke up behind her. "She likes to walk along the cliff by the beach. Especially when she wants space. But if I've learned one thing about Ava, it's that she doesn't want to be alone nearly as much as she thinks she does."

Tess stared at them. Who was Riley that they knew Ava so well? Not just her driver. And certainly not her butler. They were unexpectedly solid and muscular for a butler. When Tess ran into them, it had been like hitting a brick wall.

Wait, does Riley know what happened last night?

Tess's face grew hot. "Er, thank you. I appreciate it."

She fled back down the hall, returning to her room to grab a light jacket before heading toward the beachside cliff. It was a ten-minute walk from the mansion, and the sea breeze was cold enough that she could feel it through her jacket. But it was invigorating. So was the sharp scent of the ocean and the chirping of the seabirds breezing through the air.

She found Ava sitting by the cliff's edge, bare legs to one side and her shoes placed carefully next to her. Her hair was loose and blew in the wind underneath her wide-brimmed hat. She wasn't wearing anything over her dress, but she didn't seem bothered by the cold at all.

She turned at the sound of Tess's footsteps.

"Hi," Tess said. "Can I join you?"

Ava nodded. "Sit."

Tess sat down next to her and crossed her legs. "I hope I'm not disturbing you. I was going for a walk and I saw you sitting here." Ava didn't need to know that Riley had nudged her to come here.

"You're not disturbing me. I was just thinking. I like to come here to think. It's my favorite place in the world. It has been ever since I was a girl."

"It's a beautiful spot. Did you grow up here?"

Ava shook her head. "When I was a child, my parents brought me here on vacation. The mansion was a private resort back then, but to me, it was paradise. So years ago, when the resort was failing, I offered to buy it, along with the island."

"You just bought an island?"

"It was right after my parents died. It left me feeling impulsive. Our relationship was... difficult."

Tess could hardly imagine Ava being impulsive. "I'm sorry about your parents."

"It was almost ten years ago. And it wasn't unexpected. They were already in their forties when I was born. They struggled to conceive, but after several attempts at IVF, they had me, their only child. In a way, this island is the legacy they left me. Part of the money I bought it with came from my inheritance. But most of it was funded by the money I've made over the years through my venture capital firm."

"So that's what you do in your study all day?"

"Mostly."

Tess looked out at the ocean before them, stretching endlessly into the horizon. "So, why do you live out here all by yourself?"

"Because I prefer it. I've always preferred being alone. Or perhaps it's just familiar." Ava leaned back, stretching her legs out in front of her. "Where I grew up was very secluded. Not as much as this, but it was out in the country. I was an only child. My parents didn't have much of a hand in raising me. They were busy people, rarely home, always working or traveling. So I was left alone, with only a nanny to raise me. Our trip here was one of the few they brought me with them on, which is probably why I have such fond memories of this island. But for the most part, my parents barely gave me a second thought. Whenever we had guests at the house, my mother liked to show me off to everyone, but it was the only time I got any attention from her. And it was more than I ever got from my father."

"That sounds awful. Why did they even have a kid if they weren't going to care for you?"

"Because it's what was expected of them, I suppose. They were all about appearances, about embodying the American dream. You see, my father was a businessman. He and my mother emigrated from Chile long before I was born in pursuit of that dream. Success. Riches. The nuclear family that came with it. My father worked himself half to death, and my mother focused all her energy on being the perfect wife and climbing the social ladder. Integrating herself into high society, hosting parties, accompanying my father on work trips. By the time I was born, they'd made it. And yet, neither had the time for me."

"That seems… lonely."

Ava's gaze drifted out over the ocean. "It wasn't so bad. I had a very privileged childhood. All my needs were taken care of. I never wanted for anything."

Except for love?

But Tess didn't say that. "My childhood was pretty lonely too. My mom, she kept moving us from place to place, never staying anywhere long enough to put down roots. She'd get restless if we lived anywhere too long, so we were always on the move, taking whatever jobs she could get. We didn't have much money, but we got by."

"I'm sorry," Ava said.

"It wasn't too bad. We had each other, at least. That's what she used to tell me. It made me feel so guilty for not feeling like that was enough. Because I always wished I had a home like other kids did. And I wished I had a dad. I never knew mine. I don't even know if he's alive or dead."

"Your mother never told you anything about him?"

Tess shook her head. "All Mom told me was that he wasn't anyone worth knowing. She seemed to hate him. But at the same time, it seemed like she still had some feelings for him. She never admitted it, but I found some love letters from him hidden in a closet once. I read them in the hope that I could find out something about him, even just his name, but they didn't use their real names in the letters. They used nicknames, codenames. 'Oliver and Jenny,' they called each other. I think it was from the movie *Love Story*. Do you know the one?"

"I'm familiar with it."

"It's very cheesy, but my mom loved it. I sometimes wonder if it's because her relationship with my dad was like that. You know, two star-crossed lovers from different backgrounds? Maybe my dad was someone rich like Oliver, and they had a forbidden relationship. Maybe Mom getting pregnant with me shattered the fantasy, which is why he left her. It would explain why she thought he was such a deadbeat…"

Was she rambling? Probably, judging by Ava's expression. She didn't want to hear the details of Tess's parents' hypothetical love life.

"Anyway, I guess Mom was right about that part, because he didn't even come for me after she died. I was ten. It was a brain aneurysm, completely out of nowhere. And since I didn't have any relatives, at least not that anyone could find, I ended up in foster care. That made moving around with Mom all the time seem like paradise."

Silence fell over them. Tess turned to look at Ava. Her face was warped with sadness. And all because of Tess's story?

"I'm so sorry," Ava whispered. "I'm sorry you went through all of that. You didn't deserve it."

Tess shrugged. "That's just life. No one gets what they deserve. We have to play the hand we're dealt, even if it's a losing one."

Ava put her hand on Tess's. "Once all this is over, you'll never have to go through anything like that again. I swear it."

It wasn't the first time Ava had spoken those words. Tess still didn't know what they meant. But she wanted so badly to believe them. "Thank you. I appreciate everything you've done for me. Really."

She leaned over and kissed Ava softly. Without breaking the kiss, Ava swept her into her arms, holding her tight. It was enough to take Tess away from it all. From the island. From the world. From all her troubles.

Neither of them had said a word about last night. But

they didn't need to acknowledge it for Tess to know that it had been real, meaningful.

And yet, everything else that remained unspoken between them—the secrets Ava was keeping from her, the danger Tess was in—left a yearning that lingered on Tess's lips after the kiss ended.

That evening, Tess stretched herself out on the window seat of a sunlit parlor she'd discovered on the second floor. The sun was setting, the large bay windows giving her the perfect view of the red-tinged sky. Soon, darkness would take over, and the sky would fill with stars.

Living in the city for so long, Tess rarely got to see the stars. But here on the island, they were a regular sight, one she never missed the chance to experience.

Today was no different. However, she was far too preoccupied with her earlier conversation with Ava to enjoy the sunset. The night before, Ava had shown a little of what lay behind that stone mask of hers. And that morning by the cliff, she'd revealed even more, just in a different way.

Tess wanted more. To peel back more of those layers. To see Ava's true self. And not just in the bedroom. She wanted Ava to open up to her too. And she was determined to make that happen.

Why did Tess care so much about breaking through Ava's walls? Was it because she was trapped on Ava's island with no one else around for comfort? Was it because she was scared and alone, so trying to connect with the woman who was both her captor and her protector was the only way she could regain a sense of control?

Was it because she was starting to feel something toward Ava, something real?

In the doorway, someone cleared their throat. Tess turned to see Riley enter the room.

"Ava wanted me to tell you dinner is going to be an hour late," they said. "Some trouble in the kitchen."

"Okay. Thanks." As Riley turned to leave, an idea formed in Tess's mind. "Uh, Riley? I was just wondering. When are you going to the mainland next?"

"Probably later in the week. Why? Do you need something?"

"Yes, but…" Tess hesitated. "I was hoping you could get me some things without telling Ava."

Riley's eyes narrowed. "I don't keep secrets from Ava. And I'm not getting you anything dangerous or—"

"No, it's nothing like that. It's just some clothes, really. And… some other things."

Riley folded their arms across their chest. "So why should I keep that from Ava?"

"Because I…" Tess drew her knees to her chest, avoiding Riley's gaze. "I want to surprise her, okay?"

Riley was silent for a moment. "Oh."

"I just thought you'd be willing to help me because you helped me this morning, and—"

Riley held up a hand. "Say no more. Just tell me what you need."

Tess thought for a moment, then listed everything she wanted. Riley didn't take notes, instead assuring her that they had an excellent memory and would be sure to get everything.

"Thank you," Tess said. "I know you don't have to do any of this."

"You're not wrong. But you matter to Ava. And it's rare for her to care about anyone."

"I kind of got that impression about her too."

"She's always been that way as long as I've known her. And it's been years."

"So you're friends?" Tess asked.

"As much as anyone can be friends with Ava. Like most of her relationships, ours is primarily a business one, but after all these years, we've gotten close. She doesn't have many people in her life. So it's good to see her connect with someone. You're good for her."

"You really think that?" Tess stretched her legs out in front of her. "I'm starting to feel like we have this connection, but with everything else that's going on, it's hard to know if it's real. Things are just so confusing and chaotic right now."

"I'm sure they are. But don't overthink it. Trust your instincts. What's your gut telling you?"

"That… I should trust Ava."

"Then you should listen to your gut." Riley gave her a nod. "I'll get your things for you by Friday."

Without another word, they turned and left the room.

Tess sat back, turning her gaze to the horizon. The sun had disappeared now, giving way to the night sky.

She steeled her resolve. She would bring out the real Ava. She would get her to open up.

She would make Ava let the lioness out.

CHAPTER 14

Ava entered Cassandra's office on the top floor of the Queens Club. "You have information for me?"

The day before, Riley had gone on a trip into the city. When they returned, they brought a message from Cassandra with them. Apparently, she had important information to share regarding Tess.

Ava had flown out the very next morning. She was feeling an increasing sense of urgency when it came to matters surrounding Tess. She wanted to resolve the situation, to get Tess out of danger as quickly as possible. But more than that, the closer the two of them became, the more Ava was aware of how precarious the tower of secrets surrounding them was.

It was only a matter of time before it came crumbling down. And she needed to shield Tess from it when it did.

If I cared about protecting her, I'd tell her the truth. But could Tess handle it?

From her place behind her desk, Cassandra gestured for Ava to sit. "I have news. To start, the results of the DNA test are in. Tess Bennett is Marcus Holden's daughter. Don't ask how my PI got hold of Marcus's DNA, because I don't know. Plausible deniability and all. But I'm assured that the results are accurate."

Had Ava ever truly doubted who Tess was? All this did was confirm what she already knew.

And it gave her one less excuse for keeping the truth from Tess.

"Is that all?" she asked. "Riley suggested the news was urgent."

"There's more. And it isn't good. I found out who the men who attacked Tess are. They're professionals, just like we thought. But they're not your average hired muscle. I'm not going to mince words. They're hitmen."

Dread settled over her. She'd feared this. But she'd desperately hoped she was wrong.

"Unfortunately, that's the only information I've been able to get," Cassandra continued. "I've had my contacts ask around and try to find out who hired them, but the usual sources are being tight-lipped. No amount of money could convince them to talk."

"So we've reached a dead end?"

"Not exactly. The fact that no one is talking tells us something very important. You see, in the criminal underworld, loyalties can be... flexible. And information is a commodity more valuable than anything. You can always find someone who will give it to you, for a price. That is, unless they've been paid even more to stay quiet. And that requires significant sums of money."

"What are you saying?"

"That whoever sent the hitmen after Tess is both wealthy

enough and desperate enough to pay them so much money that they won't speak a word to anyone about who hired them. And our prime suspects certainly fit that description."

"The Holdens." They were one of the wealthiest families on the continent.

But who in Marcus's family could be so ruthless as to try to kill Tess? And all over an inheritance she didn't even know about?

"Exactly. I haven't gotten anything definitively linking any of them to the hitmen yet. I've had them surveilled, and their behavior isn't unusual. His parents are the model of a family grieving their only son. So is his wife. Neither have shown any outward signs of conflict over Marcus's inheritance, but both have had many, many consultations with their lawyers. More than you'd expect in a case as clear-cut as Marcus's death. Unless, of course, they were trying to prevent anyone from challenging his will. An illegitimate child, for example."

"How much do the wife and parents know about Tess?"

"It's unclear who knows what, if anything. Until I can get more information, this is all speculation."

Ava leaned back in her chair, weighing everything Cassandra had revealed. "This isn't a lot to go on."

"You're right. But I need you to know how dangerous the situation is. After you told me the men turned up at Tess's workplace looking for her, it occurred to me that they might be making inquiries about her elsewhere. I had my PI look into other contacts of hers. Exes, former roommates, even old foster parents and siblings. It turns out, almost all of them have been paid a visit by men looking for Tess. Men claiming to be police, who fit the description of the pair who came after her. They really want to find this girl. They're not going to stop."

"I know that. I'm doing everything I can to protect her."

"It's not her I'm worried about. It's *you*." Cassandra leaned forward, hands splayed on the desk. "These people are dangerous. What's going to happen when they realize you have her?"

"If they come for me, I'm well protected."

"You mean your island? Riley? If you think that's enough to protect you, you're *wrong*. You don't understand what these people are capable of. Not like I do."

It was rare for Cassandra to acknowledge her past. And it was clear in her expression that doing so was painful for her.

"What you need to understand is that these men aren't just hired thugs or street-level gangsters," she said. "They're professional killers, trained to take out a target without leaving a trace. They're willing to murder an innocent girl for money. You're in real danger, Ava. Whatever protection you have, it's not enough!"

"It *will* be enough. It has to be."

Cassandra narrowed her eyes. "I'll ask you again. Who is Tess to you?"

"She's someone I swore I'd protect."

"Don't give me that bullshit. I *know* you. You lock yourself away from others, keep everyone in your life at arm's length. You don't care about anyone. And you're putting your life in danger for some girl?"

Ava couldn't disagree with a word Cassandra had said. What she was doing was entirely unlike her.

Yet here she was, risking everything for Tess.

"Who is she?" Cassandra asked. "I know she's Marcus's daughter, but what's her connection to you? Don't make me say it."

"Say what?"

Cassandra folded her hands on the desktop, her fingers interlacing. "My investigations into Marcus's family tell me they used to live next door to your old family estate. You grew up together, practically from birth. Your parents were close to them, and chances are, so were you. Now I know you've never had any interest in men, but sexuality is complicated, especially when you're sixteen—"

Ava almost laughed. "You think that Tess is *mine*? I assure you, it's nothing like that."

"Then why? Why are you sticking your neck out for this girl?"

For a moment, Ava considered telling her the truth. About Tess. About Marcus. About everything that had happened 22 years ago.

But those wounds were too painful to reopen. And she had far more important concerns in the present.

"All I can tell you is that Tess and I are connected," she said. "We always have been. It's my responsibility to protect her."

"And you're willing to put your life on the line to do that?"

"I am."

Ava's words surprised her as much as they did Cassandra. She was starting to care about Tess in a way that went beyond the vow she'd made, beyond the inextricable connection between them. She couldn't keep those feelings buried forever.

And she couldn't keep the truth buried forever, either.

~

It was just past midnight when Ava returned to the island. She'd planned to be home before dinner, but poor weather had grounded her flight.

So why was Tess's bedroom light still on as Ava approached the mansion?

As soon as she was inside, she headed toward Tess's room. After Cassandra's revelations about how dangerous the men who were after Tess were, Ava needed to make sure she was still safe and sound. It was an irrational urge. The island was a fortress. No one could get to Tess. But that did little to assuage Ava's concerns.

And she couldn't deny that a part of her simply wanted to see Tess. It had been a long, exhausting day, and the events of the trip weighed heavily on her. But there was something about Tess that brightened even the darkest of nights. She reminded Ava that there was sweetness in the world, that there were people who were good.

After all, Tess treated Ava with warmth, tried her best to trust her, despite the way Ava had treated her. Dragging her to the island, locking her up, keeping her at arm's length. And yet, Tess had placed her faith in her.

But more than that, she saw Ava in a way no one else did. That night in Tess's bedroom and the morning on the cliff had proved it. Those vulnerable parts of herself that Ava buried deep inside?

Tess saw them all.

She reached Tess's bedroom and knocked on the door. "Tess? Are you in there?"

Ava waited, but no answer came. She knocked again.

Nothing.

Had something happened? All the possibilities played out in Ava's mind, each worse than the last.

What if someone had gotten to her?

She knocked again. "Tess? I'm coming in."

Ava opened the door. To her relief, she spotted Tess immediately. She was curled up in an armchair, dozing peacefully under a blanket.

She was safe. All was well.

But as Ava began closing the door, Tess stirred, her eyes flitting open.

"Ava?" She blinked. "You're back."

Ava nodded. "I'm here now. Go to sleep."

"Wait."

Tess rose to her feet. As she did, the blanket fell away, revealing a silky red dress with thin straps and a deep V-neck. It was enticingly short, showing off the silky smooth legs Ava had tried not to stare at, hugging the curves Ava had caressed and explored so thoroughly that night they'd given in to temptation.

It was *not* one of the dresses Ava had bought her. She didn't know where it, or the matching red kitten heels Tess wore, had come from. And Tess had done something with her hair, made it curl in the most enticing way. Deep pink lipstick graced her lips, and her cheeks had a rosy glow that made Ava recall the flush on Tess's face the moment Ava had pinned her to the bed and made her scream with pleasure…

Ava gathered herself. "You look… nice."

"Er, thanks." Tess's cheeks turned even redder. She glanced at her feet, her fingers playing at one of her dangling gold earrings. "I feel a little silly, all dressed up like this. I wanted to do something nice for you, so I arranged for us to have dinner together as a surprise for when you got back. There was wine and everything. But then you got delayed, and I fell asleep waiting for you, and…"

Ava stared at her. "You did all that for me?"

"Like I said, it's silly. I know that. It's just that after the other night, you're all I can think about. You're all I want. And…" Tess peered up at her from under dark eyelashes. "I wanted to make you want me as much as I want you."

And just like that, all of Ava's doubts evaporated. It didn't matter whether her feelings toward Tess were real or some kind of projection. It didn't matter if they were wrong.

Because at that moment, everything felt *right*.

Ava stepped toward her, closing the distance between them. "You look beautiful." She drew her fingers down Tess's cheek. "And you don't need to make me want you. I want you more than you could ever know."

She pulled Tess into her, kissing her hot and hard. Tess dissolved into her lips, her body trembling against Ava's. The way Tess simply *yielded* to her was intoxicating.

She wanted *more*. She wanted to tie Tess down and make her beg for release. She wanted to claim her, to make Tess hers in every meaning of the word.

But she couldn't let those impulses get away from her. She couldn't let that side of herself out. Not with the woman she'd sworn to protect.

Tess pushed her hands against Ava's chest gently, breaking the kiss. Had she been too forceful? Had Tess sensed her thoughts? She couldn't let herself get carried away. She had better self-control than that.

But as Ava pulled away, Tess reached for her tentatively, her hand hovering next to Ava's arm.

"I don't want you to stop. I want you to stop holding back." Tess stepped in close. "For once, Ava, don't hold back."

Ava looked into her eyes. They were pleading with her, begging her. At once, she was transported back to that night in this very room, when Tess had crumbled under her touch, pliant and submissive, every inch of her begging Ava to take her.

That night, she had told Tess that she wouldn't be able to handle Ava's twisted tastes. But in truth, a part of her feared Tess would reject her because of them, as so many others had. Never had Ava found a lover who truly understood her desires.

Never had she had anyone who understood *her*.

Could it be that Tess was different? That she wanted the kind of sweet surrender that Ava so desperately wanted to give her? That she wanted to completely and utterly submit to Ava's control?

"Do you understand what you're asking of me?" she said. "Truly?"

Tess nodded. "I do. I swear it."

She gazed back at Ava, her resolve clear in her eyes. Then, she did something completely unexpected.

She dropped to her knees at Ava's feet.

Desire surged through Ava's body. This was everything she'd ever wanted.

Tess was everything she'd ever wanted.

Her head bowed and eyes downcast, Tess spoke. "I want this, Ava. I want all of you. Please."

Ava closed her eyes and breathed in deep. As she exhaled, she let go of it all. Of her reservations. Of her worldly worries. Of her inhibitions.

Until nothing was left but pure, unbridled *need*. Not only her need for Tess, but her need for control.

"Stand up," she said.

Tess stood, her head still bowed. Ava took her by the chin, drawing Tess's face up to look her in the eye.

"Are you absolutely sure you want this? Because once we open this box, there's no closing it again."

Tess nodded. "I'm sure."

Ava examined Tess's face. Not a trace of doubt lingered on it. She understood Ava's words. She meant what she'd said.

Ava released Tess's chin. "Come with me. There's something I want to show you."

CHAPTER 15

Tess followed Ava through the halls of the house, the silence of the mansion at midnight amplifying the thundering of her pulse in her ears.

Why was her heart going a mile a minute? This was exactly what she wanted, why she'd done everything she'd done tonight. Dressing up. Her attempt at dinner. Serving herself up on a platter to Ava. It was an attempt to slip past her defenses, to reach the parts of her she kept hidden behind her walls. Her secrets. Her desires.

Tie me down. Take me. Make me yours. That was what Tess's body whispered to her every moment she was in Ava's presence. And she could feel Ava whispering back, whispering all the sinful thoughts she wouldn't say out loud.

Which was why Tess had taken matters into her own hands. It hadn't gone as smoothly as she'd planned. When Ava had finally returned, several hours late, Tess had turned into a stammering mess. Because suddenly, the idea of seducing her seemed foolish. All Ava had to do was look at

Tess and she would turn into a helpless puddle of lust, which was exactly what had happened.

But somehow, Tess had gotten through to her. And now she was blindly following Ava into the unknown once again.

Where were they going? Not to Ava's rooms. They were on the third floor. Instead, they headed downstairs.

From the entrance hall, Ava led her toward the back of the mansion, stopping once they reached an old wooden door, no different from the other doors in the house. Tess had passed it while exploring one day, but it had been locked, like many of the unused rooms in the mansion.

But perhaps this room wasn't unused.

Ava produced a small bronze key and unlocked the door, then flicked a light switch just inside it, illuminating the stairs beyond. They led deep beneath the house. Tess couldn't see what was at the bottom.

She glanced at Ava, who gave her a nod. "Watch your step."

Did Ava expect her to waltz into the depths of the dark basement without question? Was this a test? Of how badly she wanted this? Of whether Tess trusted her?

She took a deep breath. *Here goes nothing.* Slowly, she began descending the stairs. Behind her, Ava shut the door, her heeled footsteps following in Tess's wake. It wasn't until she reached the bottom that she allowed herself to breathe again. But with only the light from the stairs overhead, she could barely see further than a few feet.

Then, Ava turned on the lights.

Tess gasped. The basement was vast and seemed ancient, with antique brass chandeliers hanging from the ceiling and soft downlights illuminating stone walls. It was furnished like a luxury suite, with chairs and tables, chests of drawers, a lounge and armchairs, rugs and throws of fur and velvet adding warmth to the cold stone and dark wood.

But the decor wasn't what took Tess's breath away. Displayed around the room and on the walls was every kinky instrument imaginable. Whips and riding crops. Floggers and paddles. Cuffs of metal and leather. Ropes and chains, spreader bars and shackles, all manner of restraints.

And there were all kinds of sex toys, elegantly designed and looking more like sculptures, pieces of art. Tess's skin grew hot as she stared at a strap-on in a leather harness displayed in a cabinet. Why did that make her blush when there were far kinkier things in the room?

Even the furniture was designed for sex and bondage. There were tables and benches that a person could be bent over and bound to. A large wooden cross forming a giant "X" against the wall. Stocks, like something from medieval times.

The centerpiece of it all? A four-poster canopy bed, velvet curtains draped around it, pulled back and tied with gold cords to reveal a mattress adorned with dark silken sheets. And hanging from the wooden beams running along the top of the bed were heavy leather cuffs on chains, ready and waiting for a captive.

This was far beyond Tess's wildest dreams. Far beyond her darkest fantasies. Ava had a luxury sex dungeon in her basement dedicated to every erotic pleasure imaginable?

And it had been right under Tess's nose the entire time?

Ava's voice broke her out of her trance. "Not what you were expecting?"

Tess turned to her. The woman's gaze held a cold flame,

the same Tess caught a glimpse of every time Ava looked at her. But now, instead of just a glimmer, it was a roaring fire.

This was what she'd sensed in Ava, the side of her that yearned to break free and make Tess hers. This room was the physical manifestation of all of those desires, a den for the lioness within.

And here Tess was, locked inside it with her.

Ava prowled toward her. "Does this frighten you? Tell me the truth."

"N-no. I mean, it's a lot, but it doesn't scare me." Tess lowered her gaze. "A part of me has always been drawn to this. To the idea of giving myself over to someone completely, letting them take control. But I've never admitted it before. Because it just seems so… twisted. And it makes me feel like there's something wrong with me."

For a moment, there was only silence.

"Look at me," Ava said.

Tess looked up at Ava. The fire in her eyes was still there, but it had softened to a flickering candle flame.

"Never, *ever* feel ashamed of what you desire. You're not twisted. There is nothing wrong with you." She drew a hand down Tess's cheek. "In my eyes, you're perfect."

Tess's heart fluttered.

"Now, are you sure you want to do this?" Ava asked.

Tess nodded. "I've never been more sure of anything."

"Do you have a safeword?"

Tess thought for a moment. She hadn't needed one before.

"You've never done anything like this, have you?"

"Nothing this… intense. But that doesn't mean I don't want to. Or that I can't handle it. Because I—"

Ava held up a hand. "I believe you. I'm choosing to trust that you know yourself well enough to judge that, and that you'll be respectful of your own limits and won't push yourself. Regardless, I will be paying close attention to you. I will not push you beyond what you can handle. I will be in control at all times. I will keep you safe. But to do that, I need you to trust me."

"I will. I trust you." It was the first time she'd spoken those words to Ava.

And she meant them with all her heart.

"Now, your safeword," Ava said. "It's 'red.' Say red and everything stops. Do you understand?"

"Yes. Red means stop."

"Good. Come with me."

Ava led her over to the bed. Tess glanced up at the cuffs hanging from the beams above it. One from the left beam, and one from the right.

Waiting for a captive.

Waiting for me.

From behind, Ava unzipped Tess's dress, the brush of her fingertips sending shivers down her back. Drawing the straps down Tess's shoulders, she pulled them from her arms, pulled her dress down her body, until it fell to the floor, leaving her in only her bra and panties.

But tonight, Tess wasn't wearing any of the underwear Ava had bought her. The matching lingerie she had on was made of ivory lace, the skimpily cut panties barely there and the bra so sheer it was almost transparent. She'd almost died of embarrassment when she asked Riley to buy it for her. But she wanted to make Ava want her.

And the growl in the woman's voice when she commanded Tess to turn around told her she'd succeeded.

Tess turned to face her. But Ava didn't say a single word, instead devouring her with her gaze, savoring every inch of her lingerie-clad body. Her piercing eyes made Tess's skin burn, her nipples turning to tiny peaks under the lace of her bra.

Tess's breaths deepened. Ava didn't need cuffs or chains to restrain her. She was already in Ava's thrall, her willing, eager captive.

"Get on the bed," Ava commanded.

Tess crawled onto the bed, the mattress firm underneath her, the silk sheets smooth and cool against her bare skin. A white fur throw lay across the middle of the mattress, right beneath the pair of cuffs hanging from the bedframe.

Ava ordered her to kneel upon it. Tess obeyed.

"Give me your hand," Ava said.

One by one, she raised Tess's arms, securing each wrist to a cuff. The height of the cuffs left her on her knees, her arms stretched up and out. There was so little slack in the chains that she could barely move at all.

Her heart pounded, her body throbbing with the rhythm of her pulse. Everything about the situation should have terrified her. She was trapped in a remote island mansion with a woman who had power over every element of her life.

And now, she was tied up, near naked, in the woman's basement.

It was twisted. Deliciously, delectably twisted.

And so was the wicked gleam in Ava's eyes. "My sweet Tess." She traced a fingertip down Tess's upstretched arm from palm to shoulder. "How I've longed to have you like this. Bound, quivering, at my mercy."

Tess trembled. All those accusations she'd thrown at Ava, about how she took pleasure in keeping Tess in a gilded cage? They'd only been meant to provoke her.

Tess hadn't known how right she was.

"And now that I have you at my mercy," Ava continued, "I'm going to show you what it truly means to be my possession."

From a chest of drawers next to the bed, she produced a long roll-up case secured with leather straps. She unbuckled the straps and set the case on the bed before Tess's restrained body, rolling it out to reveal its contents. Inside was an array of whips, floggers, and canes, each tucked into its own little pocket.

"Tell me," Ava began, "have you ever had the pleasure of being on the receiving end of one of these?"

Tess shook her head.

"Have you ever wanted to be?"

Tess bit her lip. None of those dark, twisted fantasies of hers had ever existed outside her imagination. But this? This was real. The thrill of it made her ache between her thighs just as much as it scared her.

"Tess." Ava crossed her arms. "You've been telling me not to hold back. And you've been *very* demanding about it, I might add. Now, I'm telling you the same. Don't hold back. Tell me what you're feeling. Tell me what's going on inside your head."

Tess glanced at the whips laid out before her. "I... I want this. I've imagined this so many times before. But I've always been too scared to try it."

"That's only natural. That fear is your innate sense of self-preservation. That's the purpose of pain, after all. To warn you of harm, so you can avoid it."

Ava traced her fingers over the array of whips with loving tenderness. Heat flooded Tess's body in anticipation. Of Ava's hands on her. Of a whip against her flesh, the sting of leather on her skin.

"But I'm not going to harm you," Ava said. "I'm not going to hurt you. At least, not in any way you need to fear. You see, pain is just another sensation, like hunger, like arousal, like pleasure. And that cocktail of sensations can be intoxicating."

Ava trailed her fingers up the side of Tess's neck. Tess exhaled sharply, need welling inside her.

"But to reach that state of intoxication," Ava continued, "you must surrender. To the pain. To your carnal desires. To your Mistress's command. So I'll ask you again. Do you trust me?"

Tess nodded. "I do."

With the care of a surgeon handling her tools, Ava withdrew a small whip from the case. The braided handle was made of red and black leather, and it had a single short, thick tail that curled around itself. It wasn't like any whip Tess had ever seen.

Ava slid it through her hand, caressing the pliable leather. "This beauty here is a Dragon Tail. It's my favorite whip of all. It takes a skilled hand to control it, to strike with the desired amount of force. It's a delicate balancing act. But my hands are as skilled as they come."

Ava snaked the tail of the whip up Tess's bound body, up the front of her thigh, her stomach, her breast, the side of her throat. Tess quivered, adrenaline surging through her.

Ava leaned in close, her breath hot on Tess's neck. "I'm going to show you how exquisite pain can be. I'm going to bring you the sweetest surrender."

Tess exhaled softly, the throbbing in her core growing stronger. She could feel the satisfaction dripping from Ava's every word. Tess hadn't expected her to be aggressive and domineering. That wasn't Ava. But Tess hadn't expected her to wield her power with such cold delight either. She hadn't anticipated how much Ava reveled in control.

Ava stepped back. Tess craned her neck to follow her as she positioned herself beside the bed, just behind Tess, whip in hand.

"Eyes forward," she said.

Tess obeyed. Not a moment later, she felt the brush of leather against the back of her thigh.

She braced for the impact of the whip. All her softest, tenderest parts were exposed, vulnerable. In her bound state, her body was so stretched out that she couldn't sit back on her heels to protect herself, couldn't use her arms to shield her body. She was powerless to escape Ava's reach.

"Don't fight what you're feeling," Ava said. "Surrender to it."

Tess exhaled slowly. *Surrender. Surrender.* As Ava's words echoed in her mind, her body relaxed. She stopped anticipating the whip. Stopped anticipating the pain. Instead, she surrendered to her fate, to Ava.

She heard the snap of the whip against her ass before she felt it. The impact made her jolt, but it didn't hurt as much

as she expected. And slowly, the stinging on her skin transformed into a gentle tingling.

But before Tess had a chance to catch her breath, Ava
struck her with the whip again, harder this time, a searing
kiss on the back of her thighs. She shuddered, electricity
crackling through her.

"Can you feel it?" Ava dragged the whip up the back of
Tess's thigh. "That intoxicating rush that follows in the
wake of the pain?"

Tess murmured in wordless assent. She could feel it. And
it was exquisite.

She closed her eyes as Ava brought down the whip again
and again, each strike more intense than the last. But now,
Tess was ready. Now, she welcomed them, her body crying
out for more. And each impact was an answer to that
prayer.

She let the sweet sensations wash over her, let them
silence the fear in her mind. *I can handle this. Ava will keep me
safe.* And as Ava painted stripes across her ass and thighs
with the whip, Tess sank into the feeling, allowed herself to
fall deeper into it, knowing Ava would catch her before she
hit the ground.

That moment quickly came. As Ava struck a final blow,
Tess was so delirious that the cuffs were the only thing
keeping her from crumpling down onto the bed. At once,
Ava's hands were at her face, cradling it gingerly, the touch
of her fingers flooding Tess with desire.

"You did so well, my pet," Ava said. "You surrender to me
beautifully."

She drew a hand down to Tess's chest, sliding her fingers
under the lace of her bra to knead Tess's flushed breasts and

pebbled nipples. Tess whimpered. She needed Ava so badly. Her whole body *ached* for her.

"How about I give you some well-earned pleasure?" Ava purred.

Tess nodded, too overwhelmed to speak. She closed her eyes, her body growing weak as Ava's hands traveled down her sides, down to the waistband of her panties. She stripped them from Tess's hips, letting them fall to the bed around her knees, then slid her hand up the insides of Tess's thighs, up to where they met.

Tess spread her legs. With her panties tangled around her knees and her body stretched to its limit, she could barely part them. But it was enough. Enough for Ava to slip her hand between Tess's thighs, to part her lower lips, to tease her clit with a finger before gliding it down to her entrance.

Tess's breath hitched. Slowly, Ava slid two fingers inside her, filling her deeply. But she barely had a moment to savor the sensation before Ava began to thrust, sending sparks through her core. Her body was so sensitized that Ava's touch was electric.

A fevered moan rose from Tess's chest. She'd never made such a sound before, so wild and unbridled. But her inhibitions had long melted away, along with every thought in her head, every worry in her mind.

All that was left was pure, concentrated bliss.

As her pleasure rose to a crescendo, Ava's lips brushed Tess's cheek.

"Yield to me," she whispered.

That was all it took. Tess's head rolled back, her mouth falling open as an orgasm overtook her. Her back arched, and she pulled at the chains above her, her whole body alight with ecstasy. With Ava still inside her, her climax stretched on and on and on, until every last drop of pleasure had been milked from her.

She was barely aware of Ava freeing her from her binds. Barely aware of collapsing onto the bed, weak and spent. By the time she came back to herself, she was wrapped in silk sheets, cocooned in Ava's arms.

She let out a blissful murmur. "That was so much better than anything I imagined."

"That's the beauty of surrender," Ava said. "It can take you to the most wonderful of heights. It can feel... transcendental."

"For you too?" Because hadn't Ava surrendered tonight? Not to Tess, but to her own desires?

"Yes. For me too."

Tess planted a kiss on her cheek. "Thank you for showing me that. And thank you for sharing this part of yourself with me."

She rested her head on Ava's shoulder and closed her eyes, reveling in the softness of her skin, breathing in her scent, sweet and fresh like jasmine in the breeze. She'd finally slipped past Ava's walls. but she'd only caught a glimpse of what lay beyond them.

Tess yearned for more. She wanted to know why Ava seemed to want her and fear her attraction to her at the same time. She wanted to know about the promise Ava had made, why she'd rescued Tess that night. She wanted to know what the weight Ava carried with her was.

She wanted Ava to open up not only her desires, but her heart.

And sooner rather than later. Because everything that had brought them together—the secrets, the danger—still loomed beneath the surface. And while they could forget about it for one heavenly night, they couldn't ignore it forever.

CHAPTER 16

The fireplace roared to life, its warmth filling the drafty room. Ava rarely used the large sitting room at the back of the house, but it was one of the few rooms with a fireplace that still worked. And when Tess had mentioned one night how nice it would be to sit before a fire, Ava had arranged for it to happen.

It was the perfect evening for it. Riley had gone to the mainland to take care of some personal business, and they weren't due back until tomorrow, so Ava and Tess wouldn't be interrupted.

As Ava stoked the flames, Tess sat down on the thick rug in front of the fire. "It's beautiful. I've never seen a real fireplace lit up like this before."

Ava set the poker aside and joined Tess on the rug. It had been a few days since that night in the basement. And that night had changed everything.

Since then, she'd kept Tess at her side every possible moment. Ava had always preferred solitude. It was entirely unlike her to crave the company of another—a 22-year-old girl, no less.

And yet, Tess's presence warmed her heart more than the fire did.

Tess rested her head on Ava's shoulder, a soft sigh rising from her chest. It was so easy for Ava to lose herself in her, in the way Tess made her feel. Because it wasn't lust. It wasn't a drive to protect her. What she felt toward Tess ran deeper. Their connection ran deeper.

The other night had proved that a thousand times over. Tess understood her. She understood that to Ava, complete and utter surrender—to their desires, and to each other—was the purest form of intimacy.

That was why Ava rarely shared her desires with anyone. They were too personal, made her too vulnerable. Because in many ways, surrendering to those carnal impulses, letting go of her inhibitions, felt like a loss of control. But with Tess, that surrender felt so easy, so natural.

How could something that felt so right ever be wrong?

The two of them were bound by a forbidden secret. Their lives, their very fates, were inextricably intertwined. They always had been, even though Tess didn't know it.

But the connection they had in the here and now? It existed outside of all that. It was real. And it was beautiful.

Tess spoke up beside her. "You know what we need? Something to drink."

"I can send for a bottle of wine," Ava said. "Or something stronger."

"Actually, I was thinking more along the lines of... hot chocolate."

"Sure, that can be arranged."

"No need. I've been sneaking into the kitchen and making myself hot chocolate almost every night since I got here. Guess I felt the need for something... comforting." Tess got to her feet. "I'll go make it."

Before Ava could say a word, Tess left the room. Barely ten minutes passed before she returned, two cups of hot chocolate in saucers in her hands.

She carried them over to Ava and handed one to her before sitting down again, taking care not to spill on the rug. Tess's mug was piled high with marshmallows, while Ava's had a handful of them scattered on the side of the saucer.

"I wasn't sure if you like marshmallows, so I left yours out," Tess said.

"I couldn't tell you if I like them or not. I can't even remember the last time I had hot chocolate. It had to be when I was a girl."

"Really? You're missing out. And the marshmallows make it so much better. My mom used to make it like this when I was little. You should try it. You'll love it."

Ava studied Tess's face. It bore the same coy look she wore every time she'd tried to coax Ava into bed with her. "Why do I get the feeling you're up to something?"

"I'm not. I just want to share this with you. Will you try it? For me?"

"All right." Ava dropped a few marshmallows into her mug and raised it to her lips, the scent of chocolate mixed with the sugary sweetness of the marshmallows filling her head.

Tentatively, she took a sip.

"Well?" Tess said. "What do you think?"

"It's… good. Delicious, even."

A smile spread across Tess's lips. "See? I knew you'd like it."

She took a sip of her hot chocolate, then set her cup down carefully on the rug, leaning her body against Ava's. Silence fell over them, Tess's breaths and Ava's beating heart the only sounds she could hear. It was comfortable. Serene. Pure enough to ward off everything that plagued them, at least for a moment.

"I wish we could do this every evening," Tess murmured.

"I don't see any reason we can't," Ava said. "Whatever you want, it's yours."

"Whatever I want?"

"Anything that's in my power to give to you." She looked into Tess's eyes. "What do you want more than anything? What does your heart desire?"

"I wish I knew." Tess sighed. "When I was little, and it was just me and my mom, moving from place to place, all I wanted was somewhere to call home. And then as I got older, and saw all my friends with their moms and dads and brothers and sisters, I wanted that too. I wanted a 'real' family. But after my mom died, I realized that I had a real family all along, a real home. It was *her*. But by then, she was gone."

Tess's gaze grew distant, the light of the fire reflecting in her crystal-blue eyes.

"Since then, I've come to realize that a home and a family were just symbols of what I really wanted growing up. I just wanted to feel like I wasn't alone. Like I have a place in the world. Like I'm cherished. Loved…" She shook her head. "I'm sorry. I know that's not what you meant when you asked me what I want."

"Don't apologize," Ava said. "If that's what your heart wants, I want to know it. I want you to feel you can share these things with me."

"Well, there are other things I want. More tangible things."

"Like what?"

"I want to go to college, for starters. I don't know what for, but it's something I've always wanted. My mom wanted it for me, too. She said I had to get a degree and make something of myself so I wasn't constantly struggling like her. But I've always been too busy just trying to make ends meet to even think about that kind of thing." Tess sipped her hot chocolate, lost in thought. "My personal life is the same story. Relationships, starting a family of my own, just aren't things I think about. Because dreaming of a future that will never happen just seems pointless."

"Dreaming is never pointless. You never know what opportunities life will bring you."

"That's easy for you to say. Life has always overlooked me in that department." Tess shrugged. "I don't know. Maybe when all this is over, things will be different. Maybe I can start fresh."

Ava put her hand on Tess's. "Things *will* be different. I promise you."

When all this is over, you can go to any college you want. But you won't need college. You won't need anything. You'll be set for life. I'll make sure of it.

But before Ava could say those words, Tess spoke. "What about you?"

"Hm?"

"What do *you* want? What does your heart desire?"

Ava leaned back, stretching her legs out in front of her. *What do I want?* It was such a simple question.

So why couldn't Ava think of an answer?

Tess tilted her head. "What's the matter?"

"Nothing," Ava replied. "I simply wasn't expecting you to ask me that. No one has ever asked me what I want before."

"No one? Not even like… a girlfriend?"

"In all honesty, there haven't been many women I considered girlfriends. It's always been difficult for me to find someone who understands my needs. And the few women who did were little more than lovers. Our conversations never ran that deep."

"What's your answer, then?"

"I don't have one. How could I want anything when I have everything I could ever need? My life has always been easy. I've never had to go without. I've never had to worry about a thing."

"But that's not all there is to life," Tess said. "Having things. Having money. Sure, it helps. Lord knows that I understand that. But it isn't everything."

"Of course it isn't. But it isn't all I have. I have my home, which I created for myself. I have my work, and the freedom and security it brings."

"But what about people? Friends? Family? Relationships?"

"I have people in my life who I consider friends."

"And that's enough? Everything you have, that makes you happy?"

Ava said nothing. Because, despite all the secrets she was

keeping, the truths she'd hidden from Tess, she suddenly found herself unable to lie.

How long had it been since she was truly happy? There had been moments in her life when she'd experienced joy. Moving away from home for the first time. Graduating college Summa Cum Laude and later graduating from business school alongside Cassandra. Closing her first deal, buying her first apartment with her own hard-earned money. Sharing these victories with her colleagues and acquaintances, the few people she called friends.

But those moments were fleeting. And when they passed, the emptiness she'd carried with her for most of her life always returned.

No, Ava hadn't truly been happy in years. The last time she'd been happy was when she was a teenager, barely more than a girl, innocent of life's cruelties.

Then her world had been ripped apart. And nothing had ever been the same.

Tess put her hand on Ava's arm. "You know what? I'd like to change my answer. There's something else I want. Something my heart wants more than anything."

"And what's that?"

Tess gazed back at her, eyes glittering in the firelight. "I want to kiss you like you're the only thing in the world. I want to show you that I'm completely and utterly yours. And then I want to lie in your arms and fall asleep, knowing that I'm yours."

A smile pulled at Ava's lips. "Like I said. Whatever you want."

She took the half-drunk cup of hot chocolate from Tess's hand and set it on the floor next to her. Slowly, Tess leaned in and kissed Ava on the lips. She tasted of chocolate and marshmallow, hot and sweet and soft, inviting Ava to devour her.

Ava drew her close, returning the kiss with insistent lips. Tess wrapped her arms around Ava's neck, pleasured murmurs rising from her chest. Without breaking the kiss, Ava lowered her down to the rug. Tess quivered beneath her, the anticipation clear in her every breath—

Ava tensed. Footsteps, coming from the hallway, light but measured, deliberate. She knew who those footsteps belonged to. And she didn't need them seeing this.

She pried herself away from Tess, who sat up, confusion written on her face. But her confusion turned into embarrassment when she spotted Riley in the doorway.

As Tess averted her gaze, red-faced, Ava rose to her feet. Riley gave her a casual nod. If they were aware of what they'd just walked in on, they didn't let it show.

"You're back early," Ava said.

"Decided to cut the trip short after paying a visit to—" Riley glanced sideways at Tess "—our mutual friend. She has a message for you. I thought it was urgent enough that you'd want to hear it right away."

Could it be that Cassandra had finally confirmed who sent the hitmen after Tess? "Meet me in my study in ten minutes," Ava said. "We'll discuss it then."

As Riley left the room, Ava turned back to Tess. She'd gotten to her feet and was wringing her hands nervously.

"What's going on?" she asked. "Has something happened?"

But all Ava said was, "I need to speak with Riley. Don't go anywhere."

Tess's shoulders sagged. "Okay."

Guilt stabbed in her chest. Once again, she was shutting Tess out. Ava had told herself it was all to protect her.

But if Cassandra finally had answers, she couldn't justify keeping the truth from Tess any longer.

Riley leaned back against the wall in Ava's study, arms crossed. She checked the hallway outside before shutting the door. While she trusted Tess, she still couldn't risk her overhearing the conversation. Because Cassandra's news couldn't be good.

"Well?" Ava said. "You have a message from Cassandra?"

Riley nodded. "I stopped by the Queens Club and asked if she had any updates for you. She told me she found out who hired the men who went after Tess."

"Who? Who was it?"

"Julie Holden."

Ava's stomach iced over. Julie Holden was a woman Ava had known since she was young. She was Marcus's mother.

Tess's grandmother.

The woman had always been money-hungry. Manipulative. Ruthless. She had to be trying to protect Marcus's inheritance. It was the only explanation.

But to resort to murder? Was Julie capable of something so cold-blooded?

"Thank you," Ava said. "You may go."

Riley nodded. "If you need anything, let me know, okay?"

For Riley to show such concern, Ava's face must have betrayed her unease. She needed to pull herself together.

After Riley left the room, Ava took a seat behind her desk and leaned back in her chair, closing her eyes and breathing deeply. Her suspicions had been confirmed, her questions answered. She had all the information she needed.

She had no choice. She had to tell Tess everything.

Tess deserved to know the truth. About who she was. About who *Ava* was.

But was Ava ready to reveal that to her? Was she ready to tell Tess the secret she'd hidden in her heart for decades?

Regardless of whether Ava was ready, now wasn't the time to drop another bombshell on Tess. The truth about her family would be enough for her to grapple with. She would need Ava's support. If Ava told her everything? It would shatter the bond between them completely.

Ava would tell her everything. But she would wait until this was all over, and Tess was out of danger.

Because she couldn't protect Tess if Tess no longer trusted her.

CHAPTER 17

Tess paced before the fireplace, the heat of the fire barely reaching her. What made Ava react the way she had? What was Riley's message? Did it have something to do with her? The way Ava had spoken to her afterward, without a shred of warmth, told her as much.

Anxiety welled up in her stomach. She'd been so enamored with Ava, so caught up in a whirlwind of passion, that she'd almost forgotten the situation she was in.

Because despite it all, everything between them had been wonderful. Ava was all she'd ever wanted and more. Tess couldn't have dreamed her up in her wildest imagination. She'd opened up Tess's desires, made her feel things she'd never felt before. She'd shown Tess parts of herself that were hidden so deeply that Tess hadn't even known they were there.

But a dark cloud had always hung over them. And now, it was smothering everything else Tess felt.

The sitting room door opened. Ava had returned. And she wore a solemn expression.

Tess's chest tightened. "What's wrong?"

Ava gestured toward the couch in the center of the room. Tess sat down obediently. But instead of joining her on the couch, Ava perched on the arm at the opposite end of it.

"W-what's going on?" Tess asked.

Silence stretched out between them. Why wasn't Ava saying anything? Why wouldn't she look Tess in the eye? She was a woman with unshakable confidence, stone-faced and self-assured at all times. Tess had never seen her like this before.

"Ava," she pleaded. "Say something. You're scaring me."

"I'm sorry." Ava slid down onto the seat of the couch, but still kept her distance. "I'm trying to figure out how best to say everything I need to tell you."

"Is this about those men who were after me? Are you going to finally tell me why?"

Ava nodded. "It's time I told you the truth."

Tess waited for her to begin, the fire crackling in the hearth. It was beginning to die, but feeding it was the last thing on her mind.

Finally, Ava spoke. "The men who followed you that night after work were hitmen. They were hired by Julie Holden. She's your grandmother."

Tess's mouth went dry. "My... what?"

"Your grandmother. Are you familiar with the Holden family?"

"Not unless you mean *the* Holdens. The real estate family." They were old money, practically American royalty. "You don't mean *them*, do you?"

"I do. Your father was Marcus Holden, Julie and

Thomas's only son, and the heir to the Holden family empire. I say *was*, because he passed away recently. It was a car accident. I'm sorry."

"My dad was some rich heir?" Tess said slowly. "And now he's dead?"

"Yes. And as his only child, you're entitled to inherit his wealth. Which, I believe, is why your grandmother wants you out of the picture."

Tess shook her head. "That's crazy. Who could do something like that?"

"Julie Holden, that's who. She may seem charming and friendly, but that's just an act. She's conniving. Manipulative. Money-hungry. She married into the Holden family just to get her hands on their riches, and she's always been paranoid about anyone taking them from her. She's rotten to her bones. Her son wasn't much better."

"But..." Tess shook her head again. It was too full of fog for her to think straight. "How do you know that? How do you know all this?"

"Because I've known the Holdens my entire life. Marcus. His parents. I know them just as well as my own family. We grew up next door to each other. And I knew your mother, too."

"What?" Tess stared at her. "You knew my mom?"

"Since we were children. She was the daughter of my family's housekeeper. She originally lived with her grandmother while her mother lived and worked at my family's estate, but when her grandmother couldn't take care of her anymore, her mother pleaded with my parents to let her bring her child to live with her. She was less than a year older than me, and my parents thought it would be good if I had a girl my age to play with. Where we lived, there weren't many children around, and Marcus was my only real friend. So my parents agreed to it. Rachel moved in with us when I was nine years old."

"Rachel? But my mom's name was Alice. Alice Bennett."

"That wasn't the name she was born with. She was Rachel when I knew her. Rachel Davies. And she became my best friend, along with Marcus. The three of us were inseparable. As I mentioned, my parents were busy people. They didn't give me much attention. Marcus was in a similar situation. We only had each other. The older we got, the closer we grew. And when we were teenagers, things became more… complicated."

Ava stared into the fireplace, her gaze growing distant. The flames were down to embers now.

"Marcus and Rachel ended up in a secret relationship of sorts. But it wasn't a healthy one. I was too young to see it at the time, but Marcus was manipulative. Entitled. Used to getting his way. He was the same way with Rachel. I should have helped her, but I was just a stupid teenager myself, absorbed in my own problems…"

Ava's voice wavered. She visibly steeled herself.

"When Rachel was sixteen, Marcus got her pregnant. She didn't realize until she was too far along to do anything. The fallout was awful, to say the least. Marcus turned on her immediately, wanting nothing to do with Rachel or his child. And his parents? They were adamant that Rachel get rid of the baby, whether it was legal or not. Especially Julie. She was convinced that Rachel was a gold digger who had gotten pregnant on purpose in order to weasel her way into a wealthy family. It's not surprising she thought that, given how she'd essentially done the same thing to her husband.

"But Rachel refused to get rid of you. So in the end, everyone agreed she would put the baby up for adoption. The matter seemed to be settled. But one day, Rachel had an accident when she was at Marcus's house. She fell down some stairs, almost losing the baby. She later told me that it hadn't been an accident. She didn't fall. She was pushed. And while her memory was fuzzy in the aftermath, she remembered clearly that it was Marcus's mother who pushed her."

Tess's stomach sank. "She was trying to get rid of the baby."

"Yes. But it didn't work. The baby survived. *You* survived. And it made Rachel realize she wasn't safe."

"But that's..." How could anyone be so cruel? How could her father allow that to happen? To her mom, to Tess? How could her parents have written such beautiful letters to each other only for her dad to turn against her mom?

"Rachel feared that if she stuck around, there'd be another incident. So she ran. My investigations tell me that she had you in secret, under a false name, then went into hiding, creating new identities for you and herself, raising you alone. She didn't want the Holdens finding either of you."

"So that's why I never knew any of my family," Tess spelled out. "That's why we were always moving around, never staying in one place."

Ava nodded. "I didn't know about any of this at the time. I didn't even know if Rachel was alive, let alone you. From my perspective, she simply disappeared one day. Until..."

"Until what?"

"Until two years later, when I got a phone call from her. She told me she was safe, and she'd had a little girl. You. She told me that if anything was to happen to her, I had to find you and take care of you. That I had to protect you, make sure the Holdens never got their hands on you. She made me promise."

Ava's gaze grew distant, her eyes shimmering. Were those tears?

"But I failed her," she said. "I failed you both. When I got that phone call, I was 18, barely more than a child myself. I didn't know what to do. She didn't tell me where she was or give me any way to contact her. And she never contacted me again. I don't know why. Maybe she tried to get in touch, but too much time had passed, so she couldn't find me. Maybe you were safe, so she didn't see any reason to stay connected to her old life. So when I didn't hear from her, I put that promise in the back of my mind.

"But as the years went by, I never forgot it. Eventually, I started searching for you and Rachel, but came up empty. It wasn't until Marcus's accident that I started looking for you more seriously. I cut ties with the Holdens after I turned 18 and left home, so I only heard the news on the grapevine. It was clear by then that he was unlikely to wake up. And upon his passing, all his wealth would go to his heirs."

"You mean me," Tess said.

Ava nodded. "As far as I can tell, you're his only child. After speaking to some lawyers, I determined that it was likely you were entitled to an inheritance. I needed to find you and let you know that. Marcus himself didn't do much with his life, but the Holdens are a wealthy family, so he had his share of the family's assets. The amount of money you stood to inherit was enough to change your life. I didn't know anything about your situation, but I knew that the child of a runaway single mother could probably use a windfall. At the same time, it was my way of making up for failing to look out for you all these years. Especially after I learned of Rachel's passing. I was so sorry to hear it. She was a wonderful person. It must have been hard for you."

"It was. She was the only family I ever knew."

"And I'm so sorry you ended up in foster care. That was what made it so hard to find you. The system is designed to protect the privacy of minors, so your trail went cold after Rachel's death. But with the help of a well-connected friend, I found you. I finally found you."

Tears overflowed onto Ava's cheeks. She wiped them away, her stone expression never wavering.

"But I wasn't the only one. You were being watched, followed. I didn't know why at the time, but I knew I had to act sooner rather than later. It was lucky I did, because the men who had been following you—Julie's men—chose that very same night to make their move."

"So that's why you rescued me," Tess said.

"Yes. When I went to the diner that night, it was to introduce myself, to tell you everything. I planned to offer you the chance to come with me, the chance at a better life. I'd already prepared a place for you here if you wanted it. Everything was set. But after seeing you face to face, after all this time, I found myself with cold feet. And by the time I'd gathered my courage again, you had Julie's men at your heels."

"Wait, so you were going to bring me here all along?"

Ava nodded. "I swore to your mother that I'd look after you. I'm finally keeping that promise. I'm just sorry I didn't do it sooner."

A still silence settled over the room. The last embers of the fire had faded, a cold chill permeating the room. But Tess barely felt it. She barely felt anything.

"I don't know what to say. This is all so much." She wrapped her arms around herself. "And you knew all along? You knew all of this?"

"Yes. I apologize for keeping it from you. At first, it was because I wanted to confirm everything. Your identity. Who was after you. Then as time went on, I simply wanted to spare you the pain. But I was just delaying the inevitable. I'm sorry."

Tess could hear the guilt in her voice. But the secrets Ava had kept from her were monumental. How was Tess supposed to trust her, knowing what she did now?

Could she even trust that what Ava had told her was the truth?

"I…" Tess's voice cracked. "I think I need some space. To process everything."

"I understand." Ava rose to her feet. "I'm here if you need me."

Tess watched her leave the room, unease roiling in her stomach.

Why did she still feel like Ava wasn't telling her everything?

CHAPTER 18

For Tess, the next few hours were a blur. At first, she remained in the sitting room, staring at the dead fire, her heart as cold and empty as the darkness surrounding her.

And when she returned to her bedroom that night, to brush her teeth and get ready for bed, everything felt slow and sluggish, as if she was moving through water.

It wasn't until she was standing before her bed in nothing but her pajamas that the enormity of all Ava had revealed hit her.

She sank to the floor, leaning back against the bed. All these revelations—about her mother, her father, her entire family—crushed at her chest, choking every breath she took.

She closed her eyes and wrapped her arms around her knees, hugging them to her body. She'd never felt more alone. Sure, she'd always been alone, ever since her mother died. She'd never had anyone in her corner. But now, someone was trying to wipe her out of existence. Not just anyone, but her own family. She had nobody.

Except for Ava.

Ava had kept everything from her. Yet, no small part of her wanted Ava's comfort, now more than ever. Because from the moment Tess had gotten into that car, Ava had been her rock in an uncertain world where unknown forces hounded her.

Tess knew who those forces were now. And that knowledge hurt more than any secrets Ava had kept from her ever could.

But Tess didn't have the will to seek her out. She didn't have the will to do anything but lie on the floor and pray she would drown in the plush rug.

Tess didn't know how long she lay there for. She was barely aware of the passing of time. She was barely aware of anything until she heard a knock at her door.

"Tess? Are you still awake?"

Ava. Her cool, velvet voice had never sounded sweeter.

She knocked again. "Tess, I know you wanted space, but I need to make sure you're all right. I'm coming in."

Ava waited a few seconds before opening the door. It was only when she was inside that Tess realized how pathetic she must have looked, curled up in a ball on the floor.

"Oh, Tess." Ava lowered herself to her knees beside her. "I'm so sorry."

"This just doesn't feel real. It can't be real." A tremor shook her whole body. "My entire life, I've struggled through everything alone. I thought I had no one. I secretly wished that I had a family out there who would find me, take me in, give me everything I never got to have. And now I find out that I *do* have a family, but they despise my existence so much that they want me dead!"

Something stabbed inside Tess's stomach. She was still shaking. She couldn't stop.

Ava reached down and cupped Tess's cheek. That was all it took. Sobs wracked Tess's body, all the tears that had been building up inside erupting from her.

She curled up even tighter. "Why? Why is life so cruel? When does it end?"

Ava stroked Tess's hair gently. "I'm sorry. I should have protected you from all this. I should have found you like I promised, should have given you a better life. I can't change what's already happened, but I promise you, from now on, I'll do my best to protect you from pain. I'll give you all the things you should have had. I'll do whatever it takes to keep you from hurting."

But Tess barely heard her over the dark thoughts spiraling through her mind. "Is this all because of who I am? Everything I've been through… is it all just life's way of punishing me for existing? I'm the bastard child of a family that's as rotten as they come. You said so yourself. My dad. My grandmother. They're rotten. And I have that same blood running through my veins. What if I'm just like them?"

"Tess. Look at me."

Ava took hold of Tess's shoulders, pulling her upright. Tess dragged her head up to face Ava. What she saw in Ava's eyes—the intensity, the fire—made her heart skip.

"You are not Marcus," Ava said. "You are *not* Julie. They may be your blood, but they are not your family, and they never were. You are *nothing* like them. You're a good person, with a kind heart, just like your mother was. Do you understand me?"

Tess nodded.

"Don't just nod. Tell me you understand."

"I... I do. I understand."

Still on her knees, Ava gathered Tess in her arms and held her close.

"You don't deserve the life you've been given," she whispered. "You deserve good things. You deserve everything your heart desires. And I'll make sure you get it. I'll take care of you, Tess. The world is a cruel place, but I'll protect you from it all. All right?"

Tess nodded. Although she'd stopped sobbing, her tears kept on falling. Why did Ava's words fill her with such emotions? Was it the idea of having someone who cared for her for the first time in as long as she could remember?

But it wasn't merely an idea. From the moment she'd walked into Tess's life, Ava had protected her, taken care of all her needs, kept her safe. Could it be that, for once in her life, she had someone to rely on, someone to call her own?

Could it be that for once in her life, she wasn't alone?

Ava took Tess's face in her hands and kissed her tear-covered cheeks, one after the other. Warmth swelled in Tess's chest. She had always seen Ava as distant and cold. But beneath that facade was a softness, a gentleness.

"You're cold," Ava said. "And it's getting late. Let's get you into bed."

Tess nodded. Ava drew her to her feet and pulled back the bed covers. Tess slipped into them gratefully. Had they always been this warm and soft?

She looked up at Ava. "Will you stay with me?"

"Of course."

Despite the late hour, Ava was still in her clothes for the day, her usual outfit of a simple black dress and heels. She kicked off her shoes and slid into the bed, drawing the covers over them and pulling Tess into her arms.

As Tess snuggled against her, Ava kissed her on the forehead. The next kiss fell on Tess's lips, tender and gentle. A murmur rose from Tess's chest. No one had ever kissed her like this before.

Ava had never kissed her like this before.

And like every other time Ava kissed her, Tess wanted more. The only difference was, tonight, she didn't want Ava to pin her down, tie her up. She didn't want them to lose themselves in lust.

She didn't want to surrender her body. She wanted to surrender her heart. And she wanted Ava to do the same.

She deepened the kiss, wordlessly pleading with Ava to give her what she needed. Her hands traveled down Ava's body, tentatively at first, then more deliberately, sweeping along the exposed skin at her neck and collarbones, roaming over the curves of her breasts and the dips of her waist through the smooth, soft fabric of her dress.

She'd never dared to touch Ava like this. It was an unspoken rule between them that while Tess belonged to Ava, Ava belonged to herself and herself alone.

So when Ava drew back, Tess's stomach sank. Had she broken that unspoken rule?

But Ava only sat up, reaching behind herself to unzip her dress before pulling it over her head. Her bra and panties, made of silk and lace as black as night, quickly disappeared too, leaving Ava naked, her body bared for Tess to see.

Tess's lips parted in admiration. Ava's sleek black dresses had disguised curves rounder and fuller than she'd imagined. Beneath a curtain of dark hair, Ava's breasts were soft and full, her nipples a deep brown. The hair between her legs was dark but fine, a veil hiding treasures beneath.

Deep within Tess's body, desire swelled. Ava had heard her pleas. And she'd answered, *"Yes."*

She took the hem of Tess's nightgown, drawing it up over her head and tossing it over her shoulder. As she reached for Tess's panties, Tess raised her hips, allowing Ava to pull them down her legs. Then Ava was on top of her, kissing her, touching her, exploring every inch of her.

And while she permitted Tess to touch her in return, it was only just enough to tantalize her curiosity, not satisfy it entirely. Ava allowed her to kiss her shoulders and the swells of her breasts, to caress her hips and thighs. But when she strayed too close to Ava's nipples or the space between her legs, Ava diverted her with skillful lips and hands, teasing her most sensitive places until she was delirious with need.

As Ava's tongue grazed her nipples, her fingers stroking the insides of Tess's thighs, her need became unbearable. "Ava," she whimpered. "Please…"

Ava slid her hand up to the peak of Tess's thighs, skating it between her lower lips and over her swollen clit, sending darts of pleasure through her. But she didn't linger there for long. In the space of a few breaths, Ava's fingers were inside her, stroking and thrusting, darting and delving, coaxing out the orgasm that had been building from the moment they'd kissed.

Tess wrapped her arms around Ava's shoulders, holding on against the waves of bliss threatening to overtake her. It wasn't long before they did. She rose into Ava, her climax surging through her like a storm. Ava held her body firm against Tess's, her fingers still inside her, drawing Tess's orgasm on and on. In that sweet infinity, the room, the whole world, faded away. There was only her and Ava.

And when Tess came back to reality, it was in her arms, Ava holding her close, kissing her, grounding her. As Tess's breaths slowed and her heartbeat returned to normal, a sense of tranquility overtook her. Maybe everything would be all right after all.

Ava broke off the kiss, arms still tight around her, and offered her a gentle smile. "Rest now. I'm right here with you."

Tess murmured in wordless assent, nuzzling against Ava's body. But as she closed her eyes, she could still feel Ava's eyes on her, could see them in her mind. There was a wistfulness in them. And something else. Guilt.

I failed you.

Was that because she didn't find Tess, didn't protect her? Or was there something more to it?

What was Ava seeing when she looked at her?

CHAPTER 19

Ava sat on the lounge in the parlor at the front of the house, Tess curled up beside her, her head in Ava's lap. She stroked Tess's hair absently, her mind a thousand miles away.

Now that she had revealed the truth to Tess, the reality of their situation was hard to ignore. It settled over them like a fog, seeping into every crack and corner of the house. The danger Tess was in wasn't going to go away. Not unless Ava could eliminate it, once and for all.

But how could they fight a woman who didn't bat an expertly curled eyelash at the thought of killing her own granddaughter?

Why did Julie want to get rid of Tess so badly in the first place? Just to get her hands on Marcus's inheritance?

What was Ava missing?

Regardless of Julie's motivations, one thing was clear. She was dangerous. Ava and Tess couldn't do this alone. They needed help.

And 'the help' was the other thing weighing on Ava's

mind. Ava had sent Riley to the mainland this morning to pick up supplies and run some errands. Ava had planned to go herself, but when the time had come, she couldn't bring herself to leave Tess's side. Not after everything that had happened between them. Not while her life was at risk.

Not while she was still dealing with the emotional upheaval brought on by Ava's revelations.

So Riley had gone in her stead. They'd been due back in the afternoon. It was late in the evening now, and Riley was nowhere to be found.

It couldn't be the weather that had delayed them. The skies had been clear all day. And Riley wasn't answering their phone. They hadn't sent Ava a message through any other channels, including the secure channels they'd put in place for emergencies. For Riley to go completely silent was unheard of.

"Ava?" Tess looked up at her. "Is something the matter?"

Ava shook her head. "Everything's fine."

Nevertheless, Tess sat up. "Are you sure? Because there's something I wanted to talk to you about, but if now is a bad time…"

"It isn't. If there's something on your mind, you can tell me."

"Well, it's about what you said the other night. When you told me about my family." Tess tucked her legs underneath her. "You said you failed me. That you should have protected me. You feel guilty, don't you? For not finding me earlier?"

"I promised Rachel I'd take care of you. I didn't keep my word."

"Yes, but how were you supposed to? How were you

supposed to find me when my mom didn't even tell you where we were, or that she'd changed her name? She made it hard for anyone to find us on purpose. It was an impossible promise to keep."

Ava shook her head. "It isn't that simple. The situation was complicated."

"Which makes it even more ridiculous that you blame yourself for it. You said yourself that you were just a teenager when all this went down. How were you supposed to take on a burden like that? How were you supposed to deal with all the awful things that happened?"

"They didn't happen to me. It was Rachel who went through hell."

"But it must have affected you too. You told me about how close you two were. How much my mom meant to you. So seeing everything she went through must have hit you pretty hard."

"It was... difficult."

In truth, everything that had happened with Rachel had shaped who Ava was more than she cared to admit. Rachel getting pregnant and coming to her, scared and afraid. Rachel ending up in the hospital after the 'fall.' The threats from Marcus and his family.

And when she disappeared one day, it left Ava shattered. No one had cared that Rachel was gone. All the adults involved had swept her existence under the rug, glad to be rid of the problem that she was. Even Rachel's mother had disappeared, and no one would tell Ava where she'd gone.

She'd had no one to talk to, no one to turn to. Especially not her parents, who had never been there for her before.

She'd carried the pain of all she'd witnessed for two decades, along with the guilt.

The relentless, inescapable guilt of failing a loved one.

"What happened back then," Ava began. "There's far more to it than you know."

"What is it?" Tess tilted her head, studying Ava's face. "Is there something you're not telling me?"

Didn't Tess deserve to know the truth? But in the fragile state she was in, would she be able to handle it? Right now, Ava was the only person she had on her side. Not to mention, the only person keeping her safe from Julie. Ava couldn't risk creating a chasm between them, couldn't risk Tess losing trust in her. It could put her life in danger.

But Tess's trust in her was exactly why Ava needed to tell her the truth. The connection they shared, the feelings they held for each other, were only growing stronger.

How could she betray the trust of someone she was growing to love? She had to tell her everything.

But before she could speak a single word, the front door of the mansion creaked open. Riley had returned.

Ava got to her feet. "That's Riley. I need to speak with them."

Tess nodded, disappointment clear in her eyes. She'd sensed all along that a secret still hung between them. And if Ava didn't tell her soon, it would erode their bond faster than the secret itself would.

But Ava would deal with that later.

She left the room and headed to the entrance. What she found there chilled her to the bone.

Riley stood by the door, hunched over and braced on the doorframe. As they lifted their head, Ava caught a glimpse of their face. It was bruised and swollen around one eye, their lip split. And their shirt was covered in blood.

Ava rushed toward them. "Are you all right?"

"I'm fine. This is nothing." But the hoarseness in Riley's voice betrayed them.

"You need to get off your feet. Let's get you to the parlor."

At Ava's urging, Riley put their arm around her shoulder, leaning gingerly against her. Ava braced herself. Riley's small frame hid a deceptively solid build. As she guided them to the sitting room, Ava noticed they were limping. What the hell had happened?

As soon as they passed through the doors, Tess gasped and rushed over. Together, they led Riley to the long chaise by the wall and lowered them down onto it.

"There's a first aid kit in the bathroom down the hall," Ava said to Tess. "Go get it."

She nodded and disappeared from the room. As Ava waited for her to return, she pulled a chair over to the chaise beside Riley, sat down, and began searching them for injuries. As she tried to push up Riley's bloody shirt, they pushed her hands away.

"I already told you, I'm fine," they said. "The blood isn't mine."

"What the hell happened to you?" Ava asked.

"I was on my way back to the car after finishing off those errands. I'd left it in an underground parking lot, and they were waiting there for me when I got back. I walked straight into them. I should have seen them. Guess I let my guard down."

"Who? Who was waiting for you?"

"Men. Two of them, big guys. It was hard to see their faces, but I'm willing to bet they were the same men who were following Tess. They were definitely professionals. Even gave me a run for my money. And they were armed, but only with batons and clubs. I managed to take them out and get the hell out of there, but not without a few scratches. Gonna need a new phone since mine got smashed up, but that's the worst of the damage. If they'd wanted to kill me, I might not have been so lucky."

"What? You fought off those two men *by yourself?*" Tess had returned, first aid kit in hand and shock on her face.

Ava took the kit from her and began cleaning up Riley's lip and eye. Riley even allowed her to do so for several seconds before batting her away.

"All right." Ava set the kit aside and sat back in her chair. "These men. Why would they attack you like this? You said they weren't trying to kill you?"

"I've been in enough scuffles to be able to tell. They wanted to inflict enough damage to hurt me, but not enough to seriously injure me."

"They were sending a message."

Riley nodded. "Plus, they left a little something in the car for me." They reached into their pocket and pulled out a small phone made of cheap plastic. "It's a burner. It was left on the passenger seat for me to find. But I think we both know this message isn't for me."

Ava took the phone from them. "It's a message for me." And it could only be from one person.

She looked at Tess. Cassandra had been right. Sooner or later, someone would make the connection between the two of them.

"What's going to happen when they realize you have her?"

Suddenly, the phone began to ring.

Ava picked up the call and brought the phone to her ear. "Who is this?" she demanded.

"Little Ava. It's been so long."

Ava's blood turned to ice. *"Julie."*

"We missed you at Marcus's funeral. I'm surprised you didn't attend. The two of you were close as children. You and that maid's child. Rebecca, was it?"

Anger roiled in Ava's stomach. Julie hadn't forgotten Rachel's name. They both knew it.

But Ava refused to play the woman's games. "What do you want?"

"I want my granddaughter. I know you have her."

"And how do you know that?" There was no point in lying, not to someone as sharp as Julie.

"It wasn't easy to figure it out. You did an excellent job of making her disappear. But one of her coworkers revealed some extremely helpful information. She said that the night Tess disappeared, she received a large tip from a mysterious woman who came into the diner. Imagine my surprise when the description she gave me fit you to a T. And imagine my surprise when I discovered that you, too, have been digging around looking for Tess. You're not the only one with connections."

Ava held back a curse. She'd thought herself untouchable. She'd been wrong.

"But it was the tip that did it. I have to say, I was surprised by your generosity. Even as a child, you never cared much for people, did you? And now you've taken in my granddaughter? And for what? So you can help her rob my dead son—my whole family—of what rightfully belongs to us?"

"Do you think I care about your money? I did this to keep her safe from *you*."

Julie laughed. "Whatever does she have to fear from her own grandmother? I just want to talk to her. Make sure she understands her place in the family. I'm even willing to share some of Marcus's inheritance with her as a gesture of good faith. All she has to do is meet with me."

"Are you insane?" Ava hissed. "You sent men to kill her, and to rough up my driver. If you think I'm letting you anywhere near her, you're more delusional than I thought."

Julie let out a theatrical gasp. "You think I sent men to kill my grandchild? And to what? Hurt your driver? You're the delusional one, not me. I would never, ever hurt Tess."

"Don't play dumb with me. I see through this act of yours, and I always have. I know what you did 23 years ago, to Rachel. I know you caused her little accident while she was pregnant."

"Whatever you're insinuating, I assure you, isn't true. All I want is to speak with my granddaughter. Permit me that, and this all ends."

"And if I don't?"

"If you don't, I'll make sure your so-called driver doesn't survive the next encounter. Neither will your friends, or anyone else you care about. And knowing you, that's a very short list of people, so it won't take long."

Ice-cold rage flooded Ava's body. The only thing keeping her outwardly calm was the fact that Tess was in the room. Ava didn't need her to be any more afraid than she already was.

"Bring Tess to me," Julie said. "If you don't, I'll pick off everyone you love, one by one. And then I'll come for you, and rip Tess from you myself."

"I am *not* giving Tess up," Ava growled. "Not to you. Not to anyone. We're done here."

She ended the call. As she set down the phone, she found Riley and Tess silently watching her, Tess's eyes white with fear.

"That was her, wasn't it?" she asked. "My grandmother."

Ava nodded. "It was Julie. But I'm not going to let her touch you."

She pulled Tess firmly into her arms. She didn't care that Riley was watching. The stakes had gone far beyond the forbidden nature of their relationship.

Julie was coming for them. And she wouldn't stop until she had her hands on Tess. She would find them, one way or another.

They couldn't hide forever.

CHAPTER 20

Tess sat at the top of the main staircase, waiting for Ava. After they'd helped Riley up to their room, Ava had dismissed Tess so she and Riley could speak privately.

It was obvious what they were talking about. *Her.* She was the reason Riley was injured. She was the reason all of them were in this mess.

She was the reason Julie was coming for them.

Footsteps approached from down the hall. Tess stood up, meeting Ava on the landing.

"How's Riley?" she asked.

"Fine. They've been through worse." Ava ushered her into a nearby lounge room. "We need to talk. Sit."

Tess took a seat on a couch, wringing her hands in her lap. Ava sat down next to her, placing a hand on Tess's, stilling them.

"This has you rattled, doesn't it?" she said.

"A little. It's one thing for my grandm—for Julie to want to hurt me, but it's another for her to hurt others to get to me. I'm so sorry Riley got caught up in everything."

"It's not your fault. It's Julie who did this, not you."

"How did she even find me?"

"One of your coworkers. She told Julie's men that you got a big tip from a customer the night you disappeared. A woman who fit my description."

Tess cursed. "Ashley. I knew she couldn't keep her mouth shut."

"What's done is done. We need to focus on our next move. We need to take action."

"You're right. I don't want anyone else to get hurt. But what are we supposed to do? I know Julie wants to meet with me, but it would be stupid to trust her, wouldn't it?"

Ava nodded. "She might be trying to convince us she's extending an olive branch. But her actions say otherwise. We'd be walking straight into whatever trap she's setting. But we can't hide from her forever."

"What are you saying?"

"I'm saying we need to take the fight to her."

"Right." Tess chewed her lip in thought. "But how are we supposed to do that? She has hired killers on her side. How are we supposed to fight that?"

"With strategy, not force. I'm working on a plan, but I need more time. Time to iron out the kinks. Time for Riley to recover. A week, at least."

"Why do we need to wait for Riley to recover?" Tess searched Ava's face. "They're not really a driver, are they? Or a butler? I mean, they fought off those armed men by themselves."

"Riley is many things. But most importantly, they're the key to any plan to take Julie down. And once Riley has recovered, we'll meet with her, just like she asked. And we'll end this, once and for all."

A chill spread across Tess's skin. There was a coldness in Ava's voice that she'd never heard before.

But Ava misinterpreted her reaction. "Don't be afraid. I won't let Julie hurt you. I won't let anyone hurt you."

She squeezed Tess's hand. But it wasn't as comforting as it should have been. It was like some of that distance between them had returned, like Ava had walled off a part of herself again.

Was it because of what had happened with Riley? Or was it something else?

"Before Riley came back," Tess began, "you were about to tell me something."

"I was? I don't recall. Tonight has been so chaotic."

"It was about what happened to my mom."

Ava was silent for a moment. "It was nothing. Nothing you need to worry about." She let go of Tess's hand. "It's late. You need sleep. I'm sure things will seem brighter in the morning."

"Right." Ava obviously didn't want to talk about it, whatever it was.

She stood up. "Get changed and come up to my room. You'll sleep there tonight. I'm not letting you out of my sight."

Tess nodded. Because despite all her suspicions, right now, there was nowhere she'd rather be than in Ava's arms.

Tess lay awake in Ava's bed, staring up at the ceiling. She had fallen asleep in Ava's embrace, only to awaken suddenly in the middle of the night, plagued with anxiety. She was grateful for Ava's presence, for her arms around her, firm even in sleep. Tess's anxieties would have been even worse if she was lying in her own bed, all alone in that vast room.

She turned to Ava. The woman's eyes were closed, but her face was lined with worry, her body somehow stiff and restless at the same time. Did she always sleep so fitfully? Or was she feeling the weight of all that had transpired that night, just like Tess was?

Tess closed her eyes, willing herself back to sleep. What had happened with Riley wasn't all that was keeping her awake. In spite of it all, she was consumed by her feelings for Ava.

They'd been there from the very beginning. And they'd only grown over time. But she worried that Ava was still hiding something from her. And a part of her still didn't know if what she felt toward Ava was a product of the pressure cooker that was their situation, or if it was really…

Well, love.

Tess had never been in love before. She'd had her share of teenage crushes and flings, with girls and even a couple of boys before she figured out where her preferences lay. But she'd never stayed anywhere long enough for those flings to develop into anything more.

And even after she turned 18, and made attempts to put down roots, she never found anyone who made her feel anything close to love. Attraction? Yes. Lust? Definitely.

But *love*? Sometimes, the concept seemed entirely

foreign to her. Sometimes she wondered if she even knew what it felt like.

But how else could she explain what she felt?

Tess sighed. She wasn't going to fall back asleep any time soon. And she was suddenly uncomfortably warm, her mouth and throat dry. She usually kept a glass of water beside her bed, but she'd forgotten to bring one to Ava's room.

She glanced at the ensuite bathroom at the other end of the room. *The faucet it is.*

Slowly, she untangled herself from Ava's arms, taking care not to disturb her. But as she sat up and turned on the lamp on her nightstand, Ava stirred. She was still asleep, but her chest heaved with labored breaths. As she turned onto her side, the sheets twisting around her, a whisper tumbled through her lips.

"Rachel?"

Tess's heart skipped. That was her mother's real name. Why had Ava spoken it? Why was her mother in Ava's dreams?

Not a moment later, Ava's eyes flew open. She sat up, her hand clutching her chest.

"Ava?" Tess put a tentative hand on her arm. "Are you okay?"

Ava took a few deep breaths. "Yes. It was a bad dream, that's all." She turned to Tess. "I hope I didn't wake you."

Tess shook her head. "I couldn't sleep. I guess I've been feeling a little anxious. I was about to get some water."

"Let me get it for you." Ava extricated herself from the sheets. "I have some glasses in the ensuite."

Tess began to protest. But then she noticed how pale Ava

was underneath her stone countenance. She was more shaken than she was letting on.

Maybe it was best to let her do what came naturally to her. Taking care of Tess. Looking after her needs. Maybe that would make her feel more in control.

Ava disappeared into the bathroom, returning a few seconds later with a glass of water. Tess took it from her and swallowed a generous mouthful, letting the cool water coat her parched throat.

She set the glass down. "Thank you. Will you hold me again?"

"Of course."

Ava pulled her down to the bed, enveloping her in her arms. Tess let out a deep sigh. She needed this. And while Ava would never admit it, Tess could tell that she needed this, too.

What had Ava so rattled? Was it her dream, the one that had caused her to whisper the name of her childhood friend? Did her guilt haunt her even in her sleep?

One thing was clear. Ava still carried the pain of all those years ago. Was that why she was such a recluse, locking herself up in a mansion far from anyone else? Was that why she pushed everyone away? Because she'd lived a childhood of isolation and emotional neglect, marked by the loss of one of the few people she'd ever cared about, who had cared about her in return?

"There's far more to it than you know." Those had been Ava's words earlier that night before they were interrupted.

What wasn't Ava telling her?

CHAPTER 21

This ends tomorrow.

It had been more than a month since Ava had brought Tess to the island. A week since the attack on Riley. Five days since they had come up with a plan to confront Julie. And yesterday, Ava had called her up and told her they wanted to meet with her.

Preparations had been made. The stage was set. Soon, it would all be over.

This day had been coming for 22 long years. Julie Holden would pay for everything she'd done. Tess would get what was rightfully hers.

And Ava would finally fulfill the promise she made to Rachel all those years ago.

She walked over to the chest of drawers at the side of her bedroom. In the depths of the bottom drawer was a small photo album. Why did she keep it hidden away when she lived alone, with no one around to find it?

Because it wasn't other people she was hiding it from.

Ava's secrets haunted her like ghosts from the past, and facing them was as bitter as it was sweet.

She pulled the album out of the drawer. Taking a seat at the edge of her bed, she turned on the lamp on the nightstand and opened up the album. The photos within it were the only remaining evidence of her childhood. Photos of her as a young girl, mostly taken by various nannies. The odd photo of her with her parents, posed formally at events or for family portraits. There were no candid shots of her with her mother or father, or at all.

At least, not until she was old enough to have a camera of her own, to snap photos of herself and her two friends. The second half of the album was full of pictures of Ava, Rachel, and Marcus, spanning from ages nine to sixteen.

But she flipped past them all until she reached the photo she was looking for. It was the last photo of her and Rachel together before everything had fallen apart. Rachel herself had taken it, catching Ava unawares as she read a book on the porch swing. She'd pulled Ava into frame and told her to smile, but had snapped the photo before Ava had the chance to react, leaving her with a confused scowl on her face. Rachel, however, wore a wide grin.

We were so happy there. So innocent. Little did we know that would soon change.

Ava flipped to another photo, one of Rachel alone. She and Tess were so different. And not just in appearance. Tess had none of Rachel's naivety. A hard life had shaped her, toughened her. And although Rachel's life hadn't been easy, she'd always been a kind, sensitive girl. One who was too sweet and fragile for the awful things she'd had to go through.

But she'd managed to raise Tess in secret for all those years. Perhaps she was tougher than Ava had ever realized.

One thing was certain. It was pointless to compare Tess and Rachel. From the very beginning, Ava had worried that she was seeing Rachel in Tess's eyes when she looked at her, worried that she was confusing one for the other. But the closer she and Tess became, the more Ava realized that the two were as different as could be. And so were the bonds Ava shared with them.

There was a knock on her bedroom door. She slammed the album shut and looked toward the open doorway, finding Tess standing before it. She'd returned to her own room after dinner to take care of some things, with a promise to return to Ava's room before bedtime. But it was only 9 p.m., and she had anxiety written all over her face.

Ever since Ava had announced to her that the plan was in motion, Tess had been restless. It wasn't surprising. The revelations of the past few weeks had changed her life forever. And tomorrow would set her life on a different path, a *better* one. As long as everything went to plan.

It will. It has to.

Ava placed the photo album aside. "Come in. Sit."

Tess took a seat next to her on the bed. "What's that you're looking at?"

"Just some old photos." Ava paused. "Actually, there are some of your mother growing up. Would you like to see them?"

Tess's face lit up. "Sure. She didn't have any photos of herself as a kid. I always wondered why. Guess I know why now."

Tess shifted closer to her. Ava took the album and

opened it up between them, skipping quickly past the early pages containing photos of her as a young child. But that didn't stop Tess from catching a glimpse of them.

"Is that *you*?" Tess asked. "You were adorable!"

"So my mother would tell me whenever she was around, right before she handed me off to the nanny again." Ava continued to flip through the album until she reached the photos of Rachel. "Here."

She handed off the album to Tess, allowing her to continue at her leisure. Tess flipped through the photos, her eyes growing wider with each page.

"That's my Mom? Wow. She was pretty. And she looks so happy. So… vibrant."

"She was," Ava said. "And she was kind, and sweet, and shone so brightly. The world is a worse place without her."

Tess flipped to the page that held the photo of Rachel and Ava on the porch swing, a wide smile growing on her face. "This is such a great picture of you two."

"Rachel took it. She caught me off guard. She loved that photo. Told me it captured my personality perfectly. She was always teasing me about how serious I was."

At the time, those remarks had gotten under Ava's skin. But she'd never been able to stay mad at Rachel for long.

Not until everything with Marcus.

Tess interrupted her thoughts. "Are you okay?"

Ava nodded. "All these memories. They're bittersweet, that's all."

Suddenly, the photos were too painful to look at. She took the album from Tess, shutting it and setting it aside.

"So, how are you feeling about tomorrow?" she asked.

"Right." Tess chewed her bottom lip. "Actually, I wanted

to talk to you about that. I can't stop thinking about tomorrow. About if something goes wrong."

Ava put her hand on Tess's leg, giving it a reassuring squeeze. "Nothing is going to go wrong. I'm not going to let Julie or anyone else hurt you. I've protected you so far. I won't let any harm come to you."

"I know. I believe you, and I trust you. But that's not what I'm worried about. Not really…"

Ava studied Tess's face. "What's on your mind?"

"It's just that, being here with you, in this house, on the island… I know my feelings are illogical. I mean, I didn't really have a choice in coming here, and you wouldn't even tell me why you brought me here, and then you had Riley follow me around everywhere—"

Ava winced. "I'm sorry about all that. Really."

"I know. That's not what I meant. This is coming out all wrong." Tess shook her head. "What I'm trying to say is, despite everything, these past weeks have been like something out of a wonderful dream. For the first time since I was a little girl, I've felt like I have someone looking out for me. For the first time in as long as I can remember, I've felt like I'm not alone. I've felt… loved."

A flush bloomed on Tess's cheeks. She hurriedly continued.

"But tomorrow, everything is going to change. Either things will go wrong and I'll end up dead. Or things will go *right*. Julie will be dealt with. I'll get my inheritance. You'll have kept your promise to my mom." She glanced down into her lap, her voice faltering. "But then everything will be over, and we'll have no reason to be together anymore, and I'll never get to say all the things I want to say to you."

"Tess. Look at me." Ava waited for her to obey. "Do you really think that once everything is over, I'm going to abandon you?"

"No. Well, maybe a part of me does. But even if you don't, things are going to be different between us. That's why I have to tell you how I feel about you. I have to tell you that I—"

Ava held up her hand. "You can tell me how you feel tomorrow. After everything is taken care of. After we deal with Julie. Because we *will* deal with her. We *will* put an end to this. And when we do, nothing is going to change between us."

"But—"

"What we have goes far beyond any promise I made, any history we share. If we're going to make it through tomorrow, I need you to believe that. I need you to hold on to that. Because I'll be holding onto that too. Do you understand?"

Tess nodded. "I… I do."

"Good. Tomorrow, when all is said and done, and we return home, we'll talk. You can tell me everything."

And I'll finally tell you everything. I owe it to you.

"All right," Tess said. "Thank you. Not just for looking out for me. For always knowing exactly what I need."

Ava kissed her on the forehead. "I'm here for you. Always."

"And I'm grateful for that. Especially right now. It's like everything is just happening around me and it's out of my control. I keep going over all the different 'what if's' in my head, and my thoughts keep spiraling into worse and worse places, and—"

Ava cupped Tess's face in her hands. "Stop worrying about all that. I won't let anything happen to you. Not tomorrow. Not ever."

She kissed Tess again, on the lips this time. Tess returned the kiss eagerly, her body rippling against Ava's, her hands clinging to Ava with fevered urgency. She could feel Tess's need, but it was fueled by anxiety. She was seeking the kind of comfort, the kind of reassurance, that only Ava could give her.

Ava drew back, breaking the kiss, and rose from the bed, her hand held out to Tess.

"Come with me. I have just the thing to put your mind at ease."

CHAPTER 22

Tess gazed around the basement. The first time she set foot inside it, her heart had thumped so hard she feared it would burst from her chest. Tonight was no different.

It was only the second time Ava had brought Tess here. She seemed protective of her private sanctuary. Because that was what it was to Ava. She lived alone, in the middle of nowhere, with no one else around. Why would she need a room like this if she had no one to share it with? Why had she decorated it so lovingly, more so than the rest of the house, when no one else ever got to see it?

Because it was an expression of an innate part of herself. One she mostly kept hidden, just like the locked basement hidden under the house.

And tonight, she was sharing it with Tess again.

Ava drew her to the bed in the center of the room. "Do you remember your safeword?"

Tess nodded. "Red."

"Good. Close your eyes."

Tess obeyed. As she listened to Ava walk away, to a drawer opening on the other side of the room, she resisted the urge to look. She trusted Ava. But that didn't stop her pulse from racing.

Ava's return was heralded by the sound of her footsteps, followed by a hand on Tess's shoulder, Ava's breath whispering down the back of her neck. "This will unburden you of all your troubles," she crooned. "This will help you let go."

Before Tess could say a single word, Ava slipped something over her head to cover her eyes. It was soft and supple, and it carried the scent of leather.

A blindfold? Even with her sight, she constantly felt disoriented by Ava's presence. How was she supposed to keep her head when she couldn't see a thing? She was in a room full of tools of pleasure and pain with a woman who took joy in tormenting her with both. Would Ava cuff her to the bed again? Would she get out the whips and floggers? Would she—

Ava's hand brushed her cheek, so unexpectedly soft and gentle that a gasp rose from Tess's chest.

"Get out of your head," she said. "Be with me here."

She drew Tess into a warm, soft kiss that grew deeper and deeper until she was submerged in Ava's lips. She could feel the heat of the woman's body against hers, could taste the desire on her lips. As she stripped Tess's dress off to caress her bare skin, a pleading murmur spilled from Tess's lips.

"Patience," Ava cautioned. "I'll give you what you need, in my time, on *my* terms. Do you understand?"

Tess nodded.

Carefully, Ava guided her onto the bed, laying her down on her back. Tess waited for Ava to join her. Instead, she felt nothing, heard nothing.

No, not nothing. Footsteps beside the bed. Then a rustling sound, then something falling onto the mattress beside her, light but heavy enough for its impact to ripple across the bed.

A whip? Some cuffs? Sure enough, Ava's hands grasped Tess's wrist. But in place of the cold metal or hard leather of cuffs were ropes, thick but soft and pliable.

Ava stretched out Tess's arm, tying it to the top corner of the bed. Then she did the same with her other wrist, and her ankles, but not before stripping off Tess's panties, leaving her tied, spreadeagled and naked on the bed.

She was completely immobilized. But she didn't pull at the ropes, didn't test her restraints. Ava was meticulous in everything. Her knots were secure. Trying to break free would be futile.

But Tess didn't want to break free. She wanted to submit to Ava's control. It was easier this way, wasn't it? To give in, to embrace her powerlessness? To be freed from the anxiety and burden of choice?

So when Ava climbed on top of her and kissed her trembling lips, Tess welcomed it. What else could she do, bound and blindfolded, her body stretched to its limits?

How could she resist, even if she wanted to?

"That's it," Ava whispered. "Surrender yourself to me. Let go of everything that troubles you. I will take it all."

Her lips and fingers traveled down Tess's neck, along her

shoulders, down to her chest. She kissed Tess's breasts, teasing her nipples until they tightened into pebbles. A murmur flew from Tess's lips. *Was my body always this sensitive?* Having her sight taken away had heightened all her other senses.

As Ava slipped a hand between Tess's legs, a spark went off in her core, spreading through her whole body. Her thighs clenched reflexively, but bound as she was, it was futile. She was powerless against Ava's sensual onslaught.

And when Ava replaced the hand between Tess's thighs with her lips, all Tess could do was gasp.

Her head fell back, her feet and toes curling as she pulled against the ropes around her wrists and ankles. It was as if Ava was finding parts of her that had never been touched, delving into hidden depths of sensitivity Tess had never discovered in herself. Her lips skimmed Tess's folds, her tongue swirling over Tess's throbbing clit. But the pleasure elicited by Ava's touch only made her ache even more.

She writhed helplessly on the silk sheets. Was Ava trying to keep her suspended in this state of limbo for as long as she could?

"Please," she whimpered. "I need you."

But instead of giving in to her pleas, Ava pulled back sharply. "What did I say about being patient?" Her admonishing gaze bore through Tess's blindfold. "Do not rush me. You are mine to command, not the other way around. Don't forget that."

Tess nodded. But that didn't stop Ava from getting up from the bed, leaving Tess wet and aching.

She didn't dare protest or make a sound. She didn't want

to risk Ava's ire. Not only because she was so desperate now that she'd do anything for her release, but because she desperately wanted to please Ava.

So she bit down on the inside of her cheek as she tried— and failed—not to think about her predicament. She was tied up and blindfolded in Ava's basement for her to use at her whim. Tess could think of nothing hotter.

Just when she couldn't take it anymore, Ava returned to the bed. Relief washed over her, along with anticipation. As Ava straddled her body again, something hard grazed her thigh. And when she felt that same 'something' against the base of her stomach, she froze completely.

"Is that... a strap-on?" Tess asked.

"That's right. I've been dreaming of fucking you like this since the night we first kissed." Ava glided the tip of the strap-on between Tess's lower lips, over her clit and down to her entrance. "But I don't just want to fuck you. I want you to *beg* me for it."

The throbbing in Tess's core deepened, along with the racing of her heart. She'd never done anything like this, not while restrained. She'd never felt so vulnerable.

But she wanted to surrender to that feeling. And her body was telling her she wanted it too.

"Well?" Ava drew a hand up the front of Tess's thigh. "You were so eager just a minute ago. Now is your chance to plead all you like. Now is your chance to ask your Mistress for mercy."

"Please?" Tess whimpered.

"Now, we both know you can do better than that."

Tess stifled a groan. "Please, Ava. I'm begging you with all that I am. Take me. Claim me. Make me yours. *Please.*"

A satisfied purr rose from Ava's chest. "Sweet Tess. Haven't you realized it by now?" Her lips brushed against Tess's ear as she whispered, "You're already mine."

Not a heartbeat later, Ava slid inside her, unhesitating, unyielding. Tess sighed into the darkness, pleasure flooding her body. And as Ava moved inside her, even the darkness slipped away. All that was left was *her*.

Ava. Ava. Ava. That mantra again, that prayer to the goddess she served to bring her release. But Ava wouldn't yet grant it, keeping it just out of reach. Was she making a point of exerting her control over Tess's body, her pleasure? Was she reveling in the power she held?

Yes, but it was more than that. Ava's breaths were growing heavier, her movements more erratic. She was in the throes of pleasure too, denying Tess her release in favor of her own.

That knowledge alone was almost enough to send Tess over the edge. "Use me," she whispered. "My body is yours. *I'm* yours."

Ava's thrusts quickened. Tess wrapped her fingers around the ropes binding her to the bed, holding on against Ava's tempest, against her own growing arousal. But trying to keep herself from getting swept away was futile.

"I'm…" Tess screwed her eyes shut tighter under the blindfold. "I'm—"

A cry flew from her lips as her climax crashed through her. She arched into Ava, who continued to thrust, sending ripples of ecstasy through her. Not a moment later, Ava tensed on top of her, her cry echoing Tess's own. Their bodies joined as one, they rode out their pleasure into the sweetest oblivion, until finally, they were forced back down to earth.

And as Ava kissed her, firm and reassuring, there was only one thought on Tess's mind.

Even if she didn't survive the next day, she would die knowing she had touched the divine with Ava.

CHAPTER 23

Tess lay in bed as Ava showered in the ensuite. They'd passed Riley on their way upstairs, sweaty and disheveled, and in Tess's case, blushing furiously. But to the credit of Ava's 'butler,' Riley didn't say a word, other than to tell them that everything was in place for tomorrow and they were turning in for the night.

Tess was still anxious about tomorrow, but her anxiety wasn't consuming her anymore. Ava had put her mind at ease. That, and so much more.

How was she so in tune with all of Tess's needs? Ava made her feel understood in a way no one else ever had. She made her feel like all the twisted parts of her were beautiful. She couldn't let what they shared slip through her fingers.

Which was why she'd walked into Ava's room a couple of hours earlier, ready to tell her how she felt.

Tess was in love. It was hard for her to admit it, even to herself. After her mom died, she'd become so used to being alone, to being independent, that the love of another was something she only ever allowed herself to feel in memories and dreams.

But in the most unlikely of places, she had found it, with Ava. And once they made it through the next 24 hours, Tess would tell her that.

As she sat up and took a sip of water from the glass Ava had left for her on the nightstand, her eyes fell on the dresser at the side of the room. The photo album from earlier now sat on top of it, inviting Tess to look inside.

She glanced at the bathroom door. The shower was still running. This was her chance to get a better look at the photos of her mother. And while she was sure Ava would let her look at the photos if she asked, the expression on her face while she'd browsed them, the way she'd been so hasty in putting the album aside, told Tess that seeing them was painful for her.

Maybe it was best to take a look while Ava wasn't around.

Tess went over to the chest of drawers and opened up the album. She skipped quickly through the early pages containing only photos of Ava, stopping when she reached the middle of the album, where the photos of Tess's mother began. Some were alongside Ava. And some had a third child in the photos, a boy.

Marcus Holden. It had to be him. Tess didn't look a lot like her father, although she didn't look a lot like her mom either. Still, he had the same mousy brown hair as Tess, so unlike her mother's blonde locks. And he and Tess shared the same nose. The familial resemblance was there.

But he would never be her father, not really. Not after the way he treated her mom. He'd written her those sweet letters in secret, playing at a forbidden relationship just like the characters in her mom's favorite movie. He'd professed his love for her, over and over.

But it had all been a lie. Because he'd abandoned her mom as soon as she got pregnant. And he'd let his family hurt her.

Tess flipped through the pages quickly. She didn't want to see his face, didn't want to be reminded of the fact that she looked like him and had his blood running through her veins. Mercifully, the later parts of the album had fewer pictures of him, and more pictures of her mom. She and Ava must have gotten closer over time, eschewing the friendship of the opposite gender in favor of their own the way older kids often did.

She reached the final photo of her mom and Ava, sitting on a porch swing on a sunny day. They looked to be around fifteen. And Ava's face wore that frosty expression Tess had become so familiar with. Even at that age, she had been so serious and cold.

But her expression was a contrast to that of Tess's mom, whose smile shone brightly. Tess couldn't remember her ever looking like that. She'd always seemed tired, worn down. Had everything she went through—falling pregnant with Tess at sixteen, having to run away to save both their lives, raising a child in secret—hardened her so much?

As she turned the time-worn page, the photo came loose from the album. It fluttered to the floor at Tess's feet, face down. As she bent to pick it up, she noticed writing on the back of it. It had faded over time, but she could just make out the letters written there.

O & J. And underneath was a doodled heart.

O & J? What did that mean? Were they initials? Why did that seem so familiar?

Oliver and Jenny. Weren't they the codenames her mom had used in her love letters to Tess's father? The names of two star-crossed lovers, one rich, one poor?

So why were those initials written on the back of a photo of her mom and Ava?

The ensuite door opened with a creak, but Tess barely heard it. She could barely even breathe. *This doesn't make sense. None of this makes any sense.*

"Tess?" Ava glanced in her direction as she belted her soft white robe around her waist. "Is everything all right?" When Tess remained frozen in place, Ava walked over to her. "What's the matter?"

Tess handed her the photo, face down. As Ava's eyes skimmed the writing on the back, all color drained from her face.

"I'd forgotten about this," she whispered.

"What does it mean?" Tess asked. "Did my mom write that? Why would she write that on a photo of the two of you?"

Ava's hand trembled, the picture in it shaking. "I can explain. Just let me explain."

Tess shook her head. "It all makes sense now. This is what you were keeping from me, isn't it? All those letters I thought were from my dad... He didn't write them, did he? He was never her Oliver, was he?"

Tess looked up at Ava, pleading with her to tell her she was wrong. Because it couldn't be true. Ava couldn't have kept something like this from her.

"You say her name in your sleep," Tess said. "You look at

me sometimes like you're seeing something else, and it hurts you. It's her you see, isn't it?"

"No, that's not—"

"For once, Ava, just tell me the truth! The two of you weren't just friends, were you?"

Ava lowered her gaze to the photo in her hand. "No. We weren't."

"Then who was she to you?"

The silence that followed grew heavier with every passing moment. When Ava finally met her eyes again, Tess could see the answer to her question in them, clear as day.

"She was everything to me," Ava said softly. "We were in love."

CHAPTER 24

"**Y**ou were in love," Tess echoed.

"Yes." It was a secret Ava had carried with her for more than twenty-five years. She'd never told another soul. Other than her and Rachel, no one had ever known the truth.

Except for Marcus. He had figured it out. It was what started it all.

"So you're the one who wrote those letters," Tess said slowly. "Not my dad?"

Ava nodded. "I had no idea she kept them."

Tess's face contorted with shock. Ava reached for her, but Tess stepped back as if repelled by her touch.

"Let's talk about this," Ava said. "Please. I'll tell you everything."

She sat down on the edge of the bed. Tess hesitated, then took a seat beside her, leaving a vast space between them. And she kept her gaze fixed on her lap, unwilling—or unable—to look Ava in the eye.

Ava could hardly blame her. "I'm not going to make

excuses for keeping this from you. I should have told you everything already. You deserve to know the truth. All of it."

She took a deep breath, steeling herself.

"Everything I've told you about me, Rachel, and Marcus is true. We were childhood friends, we grew up together. But as we got older, Rachel and I grew closer, until there was something more than friendship between us. Realizing that was difficult for us. We were barely teenagers, and it was still the 90s. Things were different back then."

Ava paused. She was stalling, avoiding getting to the heart of the matter. Because that was a painful place to be.

"We were thirteen when we figured it out. It was the summer, and we'd just watched *Love Story* together. Rachel loved it, and I thought it was silly, but it made us both realize we had feelings for each other. So we started a secret relationship, using those nicknames for each other. We were teenagers in love. We thought we were being romantic. And it was a way to keep things secret. If anyone found the letters, they'd never suspect that I was Oliver or Rachel was Jenny. And we did manage to keep things secret. No one ever figured out the truth, except for Marcus."

Ava didn't know how he figured it out. Had they slipped up, or was it purely intuition? For all Marcus's faults, he'd inherited his mother's cunning nature.

"He became jealous of what Rachel and I had, so he tried to ruin it. Even at that age, Marcus was a master manipulator. I never saw it at the time, but looking back, it was obvious. He tried to poison us against each other, but when that didn't work, he resorted to more predatory behavior."

Just thinking about it made Ava's insides boil. As did the fact that she'd failed to notice what he was doing to Rachel.

"Back then, the world was much more conservative," she said. "Rachel struggled with the idea of having feelings for another girl. Marcus knew that. He preyed upon her fears, convincing her that her relationship with me was wrong. I don't know what he told her to turn her away from me, but there were threats and coercion involved.

"So he forced her to be with him instead of you?" They were the only words Tess had spoken since Ava began.

"He would never be so crude. It was more like he made her feel like she didn't have a choice. I didn't realize it at the time. I was a hormonal teenager, too self-involved to see what was right in front of me. I didn't see that Rachel was being manipulated. All I saw was that she'd left me for him. All I saw was that the girl I gave my heart to had chosen someone else."

And once again, young Ava had been rejected by someone she loved, just like her parents had done to her before. Once again, she was alone.

"I don't blame her for her actions," she said. "We were all just kids trying to figure ourselves out. But at the time, I was shattered. I'd had my heart broken by the two people I trusted the most. And I didn't have anyone else in my life. No friends, no real family. I didn't know how to handle the pain I felt. So it consumed me, blinding me to everything, to what Rachel was going through."

Ava's voice cracked. She forced herself to continue. "So when she got pregnant, and she came to me, distraught, I didn't care that she was in trouble. I was too angry with her. So I turned my back on her, let her go through everything alone. And when she eventually ran away, I was devastated. I didn't know what happened to her. She was just… gone. I was both furious at her for abandoning me and furious at myself for turning my back on her."

Guilt gnawed at her stomach. Suddenly, it was Ava who couldn't bear to look Tess in the eye.

"I tried to move past it all, but all I could do was bury it deep. And then I got that phone call from her a couple of years later. She told me she was sorry. That she regretted ever choosing Marcus over me, that she'd just been so scared and confused. That she still loved me, and that was why I was the only person she could trust with the task she was giving me."

"To look after me," Tess said.

Ava nodded. "I don't know if Marcus's family was looking for her, or if she was just being cautious. But she made me promise that if anything happened to her, I'd take care of you. I swore to her that I would. But after that phone call, I never heard from her again. I'm not proud of what I did next, but I buried that promise in the same deep place I buried everything else to do with her and Marcus. I moved away, went to college, traveled, started a career. I tried my best to forget it all."

And forgetting had consumed Ava completely. She'd put up walls around those memories, around her entire childhood. And in the process, she'd put up walls around her heart, never letting another soul in.

"For years, it worked. But as I got older, I started to see the situation for what it had been. Rachel was a naïve teenage girl who had been taken advantage of, then had been betrayed by the adults who were supposed to have her best interests at heart. And I blamed her for it. I failed her by turning my back on her. I failed her again by not protecting you from all you've suffered in your life. I've carried that guilt with me through all these years. And that's why I've been trying to make amends."

Silence fell over them, so thick that Ava could feel it. Any catharsis she felt from finally speaking the truth was overshadowed by her shame.

And when she looked into Tess's eyes and saw the pain in them, a knife twisted in her heart.

"All of this," Tess said quietly. "Everything you've done for me. It's because you felt guilty for abandoning my mom when she needed you? For leaving her at the mercy of Marcus and his family?"

"Yes, but—"

"So everything you said about wanting to protect me was a lie? You never gave a damn about me. Only *her*. And your own guilt."

"No, that's not what I'm saying. Tess, I *do* care about you. You have no idea how much I care about you."

"You expect me to believe that?" Tess shook her head. "All of this. Everything we've shared. It was just you reliving your fucked up teenage romance with her!"

Ava recoiled. "That's not what this is. You have to believe me."

"Why should I? Why should I believe you when you've been lying to me about everything from the start? You told me to trust you, and I did. You told me you'd tell me everything, and I believed you. But all you did was keep me in the dark and lie to me!"

"Tess—"

"No." She rose to her feet, her hands curling into fists at

her sides. "Why should I listen to another word out of your mouth? Why should I trust anything you say?"

But what could Ava say to that? She was right.

Tess should never have trusted her.

Tess scoffed. "Yeah. That's what I thought."

Resignation burning in her eyes, she turned and marched toward the door. Ava didn't try to stop her. Not until her hand was on the door handle.

"Tess, wait."

Tess paused, her back to Ava. "What? What is it? More lies?"

"No. I just want to say…"

Ava hesitated. Tess didn't turn around, but for a moment, her posture loosened, her shroud of anger slipping. It was as if she were waiting for Ava to do something, say something, that would make it all okay.

Tell her. Tell her how you feel.

"It's… about tomorrow," Ava said. "It's too late to change our plans. We need to meet with Julie."

Tess stiffened. And just like that, the moment was lost.

"Are you asking me, or telling me?" Tess said, her voice dripping with disdain. "You know what? Don't answer that. It's not like you've ever given me a choice in any of this before." She turned to face Ava, her gaze devoid of all warmth. "I'll be ready first thing in the morning. I'll go through with the plan. And when it's all over, I'll finally get away from this god-forsaken house, this god-forsaken island. And from *you*."

Tess wrenched the door open. As she stepped through it and slammed it behind her, she didn't look back.

CHAPTER 25

When morning rolled around, Tess had barely slept. Nevertheless, she got out of bed and prepared herself for the day. For ending her ordeal, once and for all. For facing Julie Holden.

For leaving Ava behind her.

How could Tess have ever trusted her? How could she have fallen in love with her, and believed for a moment that Ava loved her in return? She'd brought Tess to the island against her will, locked her up inside her mansion, kept her in the dark for weeks. And even after revealing everything to her, she'd continued to lie and deceive her.

Ava had never cared about her. She'd never *wanted* her. What Ava wanted was a woman long gone, a ghost. And she had used Tess as a replacement.

It was cruel. But why should Tess believe that Ava was ever anything *but* cruel? She'd shown who she was the day she'd picked Tess up off the street and forced her onto that plane, all under the guise of protecting her.

And she'd had no reservations about starting a twisted,

kinky affair with Tess, where she was nothing more than Ava's toy, to do as she pleased with...

No, that wasn't fair. It had been Tess who had thrown herself at Ava. Sure, she'd been alone, confused, scared. But her attraction to Ava had always been there. Her feelings toward Ava had always been real. And Ava had never made her feel used. She'd always made Tess feel cherished, loved.

But a cherished toy was still just that—a possession.

There was a knock on Tess's door. She tensed, bracing herself for Ava's voice, the voice she'd once found so alluring.

But instead, Riley's deeper tones reverberated through the door. "Tess, are you awake? If you want breakfast, we're leaving in half an hour."

"I'm good." She couldn't stomach food this morning. "I'll be down soon."

But she waited until the last moment to leave her room. And when she did, Ava was nowhere to be found. The only other person in the vast, empty mansion was Riley, who waited for her by the front door.

They gave her a nod as she descended the grand staircase. "Are you ready?"

Tess nodded. "Let's go."

As she stepped through the front door for the final time, she turned to give the old house one last look. In spite of it all, the mansion had started to feel like home.

But Tess knew better than to get attached to any place, or anyone. Nothing ever lasted. Especially nothing good.

She shut the door and began the march down to the airstrip, Riley at her side.

It wasn't until they emerged from the trees flanking the

winding path that she spotted Ava. She was dressed in a long black coat that flowed down her body, her long hair whipping in the wind under her hat, dark glasses protecting her eyes from the morning sun. Or did she wear them so she wouldn't have to look at Tess? So Tess wouldn't see the betrayal in her eyes?

Ava turned toward them as they approached. "You're here. Are you ready?"

Riley nodded. Tess remained silent.

"You both know the plan?" Ava asked. "Do you have everything you need?"

"I'm all set," Riley said.

"And you, Tess? Once we get on the plane, there's no turning back."

Tess nodded. There was nothing she wanted to say to Ava.

But Ava stood there, waiting. Waiting for Tess to speak. Waiting for her to break the tension between them. Waiting for her to show some sign of forgiveness.

All Tess said was, "Can we go already?"

Ava's sunglasses made her already inscrutable face even harder to read. But Tess didn't need to read the woman's expression to see the way her heart wrenched at Tess's words.

Guilt tore at her stomach. She ignored it. She had more important things to worry about. Like facing her grandmother, a woman who had already tried to kill her on multiple occasions. If the plan went right, Tess's life would be changed forever. If the plan went *wrong*?

She wouldn't have a life to worry about at all.

She marched toward the plane at the other end of the airstrip, Ava and Riley behind her.

This was the end, one way or another.

~

"We're here." Ava glanced over her shoulder at Tess from her place in the driver's seat. "My childhood home."

Tess avoided her gaze, instead staring out the window as they passed through the iron gates flanking the road leading into the country estate. Ava had told her it was abandoned years ago, and it showed. The grounds were wild and over-grown, overtaken by nature.

As was the manor itself. As they drove up the long drive-way, the sprawling, weather-worn facade came into view. But they weren't headed inside the house. Instead, they'd agreed to meet Julie in the courtyard, just the three of them, alone. When Julie had insisted on meeting somewhere private, Ava had insisted on this location. The fact that she'd agreed to meet them on Ava's home turf was a sure sign that Julie believed she had the upper hand.

She was planning something. But so was Ava.

They were prepared. Everything was under control. Yet Tess couldn't settle the unease in her stomach as Ava parked the car in the driveway.

She turned off the engine and got out of the car. Tess followed. They made their way toward the courtyard in silence, the only sounds the chirping of birds and the anxiety thundering inside Tess's mind. It had only been last night that she'd gone to Ava, determined to tell her how she felt. Now, Tess wasn't even sure what she felt.

But what if she never got the chance to figure that out? Could she really leave things up in the air between them?

She glanced at Ava. Her sunglasses covered her face, but she kept a brisk pace, her posture alert, on the lookout for any signs of trouble. They'd arrived early, but it was clear Ava wasn't taking any chances.

They reached the courtyard. It had multiple entrances leading into the surrounding manor, all locked. Only one entrance, the one they had come through, led outside. It was among the reasons Ava had chosen the location. One way in. One way out.

As Ava surveyed their surroundings carefully, Tess examined the plants and old statues that filled the courtyard. The gardens here were less overgrown. Perhaps Ava had hired someone to do minimal maintenance.

She returned to where Tess stood, phone in hand. "That's Riley. They're in position."

Tess nodded.

"How are you feeling about all this?"

"Fine," Tess murmured. But she couldn't hide her unease. "A little nervous, actually."

Ava slipped her phone into her coat pocket. "I'd be surprised if you weren't. Just remember to stick to the plan. And don't believe anything Julie says. Her words are all lies."

Just like yours? But Tess didn't say that out loud. Because she wasn't sure she even believed it. She didn't know what to believe anymore.

"Tess." Ava removed her sunglasses to look into her eyes. "I know you have no reason to trust me. But every time I said I wouldn't let any harm come to you, I meant it. Every time I said I'd protect you, *I meant it.* So even if you don't trust me, believe me when I say that I won't let Julie hurt you."

She'd kept Tess in the dark. She'd kept secrets from her. But the conviction in Ava's eyes? The steadfastness of her gaze? They were genuine.

"I... I believe you," Tess said. "I don't know why, but I do. And despite it all, my heart *still* tells me to trust you. Which is why I don't want to leave things between us like this."

"Neither do I. Tess, I know keeping the truth from you was wrong. I told myself I was doing it to spare you the pain, but that was a lie. I kept the truth from you because I didn't want to confront everything I've been feeling. All this time, I've been battling my guilt. Not only over failing you and Rachel. But because the moment I met you... the moment I laid eyes on you... I started falling for you."

Tess's heart thrummed inside her chest. Ava had never spoken about her feelings in such an honest, vulnerable way.

"And the truth is, at first I thought those feelings were projection. I worried it was her I was falling for, not you. That's why I resisted them. That's why I kept trying to push you away. But my feelings for you were just too strong. And when I gave in to them, I realized I was wrong. It wasn't her I saw when I looked at you. It never was. It was you."

She took Tess's hand. "Yes, everything I did in seeking you out was for Rachel. But that all changed when I met you. I knew I had to protect you, not because of the promise I made, but because it was what my heart wanted. And the moment you kissed me, you captured my heart. *You* did. It was always you."

Tess's stomach fluttered. She wanted so badly to believe Ava.

But before either of them could say another word, Ava's phone pinged in her coat pocket.

She took it out. "It's from Riley. Julie is here."

The butterflies in Tess's stomach turned to concrete. Ava slipped the phone back into her coat pocket and straightened it out. Every hint of softness she'd shown in the past few minutes was gone.

In its place was cold, hard steel.

"Get ready," she said. "And remember what I told you. *Do not* trust her."

Tess held her breath as they waited. Minutes passed, but they felt like hours.

Finally, a woman appeared at the entrance to the courtyard. Tall, with a platinum-blonde bun at the back of her head, wearing a long fur coat, looking as regal as she was beautiful.

Julie Holden. Tess's grandmother. The woman who wanted her dead.

Julie's lips grew into a wide smile, her dark, hypnotic eyes settling on her only grandchild.

"Hello, Tess."

CHAPTER 26

D*o not trust her.*
Those had been Ava's final words to Tess for a good reason. Ava had never trusted Julie Holden, even as a child. She was manipulative. Seductive, almost.

Dangerous.

Seeing her in the flesh, dark eyes fixed on Tess like a cheetah stalking a gazelle, only reminded Ava of that. So did the way Tess stared back at her, frozen in place, mesmerized.

Ava stepped closer to Tess. Inside, she was screaming to get her far away from here, away from danger. She wanted to take Tess's hand and run, to hold her close and shield her from the predator that was Julie.

But they couldn't run. They couldn't keep hiding.

They had to face her.

Ava turned to the woman, her gaze hard as stone. "Julie."

A smile grew across Julie's lips, but it didn't reach her eyes. "Ava Vidal. It's been so long since I've seen your face.

And it's been so long since I've been back here. It's like stepping into the past, isn't it?"

"We didn't come here to make small talk. Let's cut to the chase."

Julie tutted. "Where *are* your manners? I know your parents taught you better than that. Have you no respect for your elders?"

"Only those who are deserving of it."

Julie brought a manicured hand to her chest. "You wound me. I know you see me as some kind of monster, but you're mistaken. What happened with your little friend all those years ago, the maid's daughter—"

"Rachel," Ava said firmly. "Her name was *Rachel*."

"Yes, yes. What happened with her was unfortunate, but you have the wrong idea. You were too young to understand what was really going on."

"I may have been young, but I understood everything. I understood the harm you caused Rachel. And I understand your intentions toward Tess."

"There's no need for such hostility. But it's admirable how you're looking out for Tess. I know how close you and Rachel were. Such good, loyal *friends*."

She knows. Did Marcus tell her or did she figure it out herself?

Ava pushed the thought aside. The past was in the past. She had more important things to focus on in the present.

Like the way that Julie was inching toward them.

"I assure you," she continued, "I have no ill intentions toward Tess. I simply want to talk to her."

Ava took another protective step toward Tess. But it was all she would allow herself. She couldn't betray the true nature of their relationship to Julie. She would surely use it against them.

"She's my granddaughter, after all," Julie said. "I would never harm a hair on her head."

"Do you really think we're that naive? You already tried to kill her!"

But Julie ignored her, addressing Tess directly. "Please believe me. I would never, ever hurt you. I know this woman has poisoned you against me, but none of what she's saying is true." She clutched at her breast with her hand. "You're family, Tess. And I've been searching for you for so long."

Ava looked at Tess. She was staring back at Julie, entranced by the woman's eyes.

"Y-You were looking for me?" They were the first words she'd uttered since Julie arrived.

"Oh yes. I've been trying to find you your whole life. Tess, you're my one and only grandchild. You're my own flesh and blood. Marcus's death only made me realize how important that is. You're a Holden, and you deserve everything that entails. Money. Power. An easy life. You deserve to have a family. I want to give that to you."

"Don't listen to her," Ava said.

But Tess barely seemed to hear her. She seemed captivated by Julie's words.

"I know what life has been like for you," Julie continued. "On the run with your mother, moving from place to place, living out of trailers, then dozens of different foster homes after your mother died. Always struggling. Always alone. Never having a place to call home. It didn't have to be that way. It doesn't have to be that way anymore." She held out her hand. "Come with me, and I'll make sure you have the life you deserve. I'll give you a real family. A home."

Ava looked from one woman to the other. Was Tess falling for this act? Did she truly believe Julie's lies?

Ava had to do something.

"Tess," she said. "This isn't what you want. You told me that, remember? That night, in front of the fireplace. You told me your heart's desire."

Tess's gaze flitted between Julie and Ava. Ava didn't dare speak the words Tess had spoken to her that night, but she heard them in her mind, clear as crystal, along with all that had gone unspoken.

I want to feel like I'm not alone. Like I have a place in the world. Like I'm cherished. Loved.

I want to lie in your arms and fall asleep, knowing that I'm yours.

"I want that too," Ava said. "I want all of that, with you."

Tess's lips parted silently, her gaze settling on Ava.

And just like that, Julie's spell was broken.

"You're... you're right." Tess shook her head. "I don't want that. I don't want to be a Holden. I don't want to be part of your family. I already have somebody who cares about me." She locked eyes with Julie. "And even if I didn't, I would never, *ever* trust you."

For a moment, Julie seemed hurt, her pained expression almost enough to fool even Ava.

But the moment didn't last. Because a second later, her lips curled into a snarl.

"That's a pity," she said. "You could have had it all. You could have had everything, if you'd just been a good little girl and done what you were told. Your mother was the same. If she'd just gotten rid of you like we told her to, we wouldn't be in this mess. Or if she'd kept her legs shut in the first place."

"Don't talk about Rachel like that," Ava growled.

Julie ignored her. "But she didn't, so now I'm stuck cleaning up this mess. Just know that it didn't have to be this way. *You* did this, both of you."

"What the hell are you talking about?"

"Little Ava. Did you actually think I'd let you walk away from this?"

"But you swore it. You swore you wouldn't hurt her!"

"What's a little white lie when it comes to protecting what's mine? Marcus's money belongs to his family, to *me*. Where do you think he got it from in the first place? The man never worked a day in his life! But my husband's financial advisers convinced him it was prudent to hold some of our assets in our son's name. I told my husband it was a bad idea, but did he listen to me? Of course he didn't!"

Ava glanced sideways at Tess. She seemed oblivious to what Ava could see plain as day. Cracks that were appearing in Julie's facade, her gaze growing more and more erratic. She was losing her composure.

And that made her unpredictable.

"We gave that ungrateful bastard millions!" she said. "And we made sure that vapid trophy wife of his couldn't touch it, made sure that if anything were to happen to him, it would all come back to us. But apparently, he added a clause to his will that gave everything to his children if he died. I'm assuming he meant the children he was planning to have with his wife. The idiot didn't consider that he already had an illegitimate daughter running around!"

"I understand why you're upset," Ava began. "But you don't need to come after Tess like this. You never did. She didn't even know about her inheritance when you sent those men after her. She didn't know who her father was."

"You think her gold-digging whore of a mother didn't tell her about her rich father?" Julie spat. "You think I'm going to sit back and let some bastard take everything from me, leaving me destitute?"

"What are you talking about? You and your husband are worth billions."

Julie spoke through gritted teeth. "We *were* worth billions. But my husband made some poor financial decisions over the years, including a teensy bit of tax evasion. Well, the IRS has come knocking, and they want everything. Even our home. We'll be left with pennies!" She threw her hands up. "I will *not* be left homeless, rotting on the streets until the end of my days, all because of my husband's actions!"

"So you're broke."

That was why Julie was so desperate. That was why she'd tried to have Tess killed. Julie Holden was a woman driven by greed, having clawed her way up the social ladder, marrying into a wealthy family and living like a queen. Now, she faced losing everything.

And there was nothing more dangerous than someone with nothing left to lose.

Ava held up her hands in conciliation. "I'm so sorry all this is happening to you. Truly. But you don't have to do this. You can have Marcus's money. No one but the three of us knows that Tess is his daughter. No one else ever has to know. Rachel did a good job of hiding Tess's existence from everyone, cutting off any ties she had with your family. If you let us walk away from here, we'll never tell a soul."

Julie scoffed. "You expect me to believe that?"

"We don't care about the money. Tess is under my protection now. I have enough money of my own. She has no reason to go after yours or tell anyone about her parentage."

Julie shook her head. "I'm sorry, but I just can't take that chance. I have to be certain she won't be able to get her claws into what's mine."

"You'd do that? You'd kill your own granddaughter?"

"She was never supposed to be born in the first place! I did my best to make sure she wasn't, but I failed."

"So it really was you who caused Rachel's accident?" Ava asked. "You pushed her down the stairs to try to get rid of her baby?"

"I should have tried harder back then. Do you have any idea how hard it is to have someone killed? My men had Tess in their sights until you snatched her away."

"So you admit it? You sent those hitmen after Tess?"

"*Hitmen* sounds so crass. But yes, I did. Their job was to make her disappear without a trace. And they would have succeeded that night if it wasn't for you. But now is my chance to finally finish what I started."

Ava's hands curled into fists. "How can you be so heartless? Do you really have it in you to kill an innocent girl?"

"Of course not. I won't be the one doing the deed. I don't like to get my hands dirty. The moment you leave this courtyard, you'll be faced with a team of men who will take you off to quietly dispose of you. Both of you. Because I can't have our little secret getting out, can I?"

"But you said you'd come alone." Ava let her voice shake as she spoke. "You *promised*."

"Like I said, what's a little white lie when it comes to protecting your own? It isn't only about the money. The Holden family name—our very reputation—is at stake. You'd understand if you had a family of your own."

Ava closed her eyes, taking a deep breath. When she opened them, it was with a sense of cold, calculating calm that rivaled Julie's.

"That's where you're wrong," she said.

"I beg your pardon?"

"That's where you're wrong. I may not have a family, but I understand what it's like to want to protect those I love. To do anything for them. Even *lie*."

Julie's impeccable confidence wavered. It was almost imperceptible, but Ava saw it.

"You didn't come alone," she continued. "And neither did I. Did you actually think I'd waltz in here with Tess, completely unprotected? I know you. You think you're above having to play by the rules. You had a plan all along. And I also know you don't like to get your hands dirty. I knew you'd bring backup to take care of any messy business for you. So I brought backup of my own."

Julie scoffed. "You think you can bluff your way out of this? My team has been camped out waiting for you since before you arrived. They'd have noticed if you had men of your own lurking."

"Oh, Julie. We both know that I've never been one for men. And my backup is only one person."

"One person? What are you talking about?"

"Remember Riley? My driver? The one you used to send

me a message? They were very pissed off about that. Pissed off enough to want revenge."

"Ah, yes. Your 'driver.' I looked her up after she gave my men a run for their money. Her background was quite interesting. Do you always hire ex-Special Forces soldiers as drivers?"

"Only when I need protection from people like you."

"Well, all her experience won't help you now. She's no match for an entire team."

"Wrong again. The entire time we've been talking, Riley has been picking off your men, one by one. They should be finished by now. Let me check."

Ava took her phone from her pocket. Sure enough, she'd received a message from Riley giving her the thumbs up and signaling in the agreed-upon code that they were on their way to the courtyard.

"Looks like they're done."

Julie's face paled. "That's impossible." She reached into her purse and withdrew a small earpiece, sticking it in her ear. "Hello? Do you read me? Are you there?"

The silence that followed was the only confirmation Ava needed. No one was coming to Julie's rescue.

It was time to end this.

"It's over, Julie. Here's what's going to happen. We're going to leave here. So are you. We're all going to forget any of this happened. We won't come after you, and you won't come after us."

That was a lie. There was no way in hell Ava was letting Julie go free. But Julie didn't need to know that.

Julie's lips curled up in an icy smile. "I'm afraid that's not going to happen."

Ava's blood ran cold. The dark look in Julie's eyes told her all she needed to know.

Julie had outmaneuvered her.

What had Ava missed? With Riley's help, she'd considered every possibility, planned for every contingency. She'd seen the trap coming a mile away, had predicted every one of Julie's moves. She and Tess had strung Julie along, stalled for long enough to give Riley time to eliminate her men.

What did I miss?

"I wasn't lying when I told you I don't like to get my hands dirty," Julie said. "But just because I don't like it, that doesn't mean that I won't."

Once again, Julie reached into her purse.

This time, she pulled out a small handgun.

She pointed the gun at Tess.

"It's time I finished you off myself."

CHAPTER 27

Ava froze in place. She hadn't prepared for this. Julie Holden had always worked by proxy. Manipulating or paying others to do her work. Orchestrating scenarios that served her goals, like the accident that had ended with Rachel at the bottom of the stairs. Julie was above doing such deeds herself.

Or so Ava had thought. She'd underestimated the depths of the woman's desperation.

Would that mistake cost Tess her life?

"You'd murder us in cold blood?" Ava said. "Your own grandchild?"

"Anything to protect my family," Julie replied. "My *real* family."

"Don't you mean yourself? Because that's all you ever cared about, Julie. And that's all you have left."

She pointed the gun at Ava. That was what Ava wanted. She needed Julie to see her as the bigger threat. The longer her attention was on Ava, the longer Tess had.

But they couldn't keep stalling. Julie wouldn't fall for that trick again. They had nothing left in their arsenal.

They were out of time.

Ava looked at Tess out of the corner of her eye. She was pale as a ghost. But Ava didn't dare spare more than a glance at her. She couldn't risk taking her eyes off a crazed, desperate Julie.

Ava had no choice. If she was to give Tess a fighting chance, she needed to take Julie out. Unarmed, Ava was no match for her, but she would try all the same. Even if it meant simply giving Tess an opening to run away. Even if it meant holding Julie off for long enough for Riley to come to Tess's rescue. Even if it meant giving her life.

Ava would do anything to protect the woman she loved.

"Wait!" Tess's cry echoed through the courtyard.

Julie turned her head in Tess's direction, the gun still trained on Ava. "Don't worry, dear. I'll get to you next."

"No, please! Don't do this!" Tess's voice quivered, her eyes shimmering with tears. "I'll go with you. I'll do whatever you say!"

Julie's finger tightened on the trigger of the gun. "It's far too late for that, Tess."

"Please! Please don't hurt her."

Julie hesitated.

There. A crack in her resolve.

This was Ava's chance.

She launched herself at Julie, throwing her whole body against the woman. As they collided, the gun went off with a bang. Tess's scream rang in Ava's ears, almost as deafening as the gunshot.

But the bullet had missed its target. Ava was unscathed,

and Tess was unhurt, having ducked behind a large statue. As Julie raised the gun again, there was only one thought on Ava's mind.

Keep Tess safe.

"Tess," she said. *"Run."*

Ava didn't wait to see if she obeyed before locking her hands on Julie's shoulders and pushing hard, sending her tumbling over the stone garden edging behind her. Julie toppled backward, dragging Ava down with her. As they hit the ground, the gun fell from Julie's hand, sliding just out of reach of both of them. Julie lunged for it, but Ava pinned her wrist to the hard stone ground, trapping the woman's body beneath her own.

But Julie wasn't giving up that easily. She wrenched her hand from Ava's grasp and flung herself upward at Ava, grappling and punching wildly. As her fist collided with the side of Ava's face, Julie threw her to the side, smashing Ava's head against the stone edging.

White-hot pain flared in Ava's head. Her vision darkened, her ears ringing.

As the world returned to focus, she found Julie on top of her, one hand clawing at Ava's face, the other around her throat.

Her head spinning, Ava battered her fists against the woman, but Julie shrugged off every blow. How was a 60-year-old so strong? It was as if her desperation had given her superhuman strength.

But Ava had something driving her too. A desire to protect Tess. A desire to give her the world.

A desire to sit by the fire with the woman she loved, knowing that their hearts belonged to each other.

Julie's hand still clutching her throat, Ava sucked in a breath, summoning clarity. She needed to end this, now. The gun lay right beside them, just out of reach.

But it wasn't the only weapon nearby.

Ava stretched out her arm, reaching not for the gun but for a small stone statuette that sat in the garden bed beside them. As her vision began to fade, her hand curled around it.

Yes! Gathering what remained of her strength, she grabbed hold of the statuette and lifted it into the air, striking Julie on the side of her head.

It hit with a solid thud. Julie faltered, her grip around Ava's neck loosening. But she didn't let go. Ava struck her again, once, twice, three times, until finally, Julie's arms slackened and her body went limp, collapsing on top of Ava.

Ava drew in a deep, trembling breath.

It was over.

She rolled Julie aside. The woman was out cold. Ava rose to her feet. Her body was bruised and her head ached, but all she wanted was to find Tess and make sure she was unhurt.

However, it was Tess who found her, rushing toward her with arms outstretched.

"Didn't I tell you to run?" Ava said.

"Did you really think I'd leave you?" She threw her hands around Ava's neck. "Oh, Ava. I thought I was going to lose you!"

Ava embraced her for a moment before pulling back. "Are you all right? Are you hurt?"

"Me? What about you? She shot at you! And your head. You're bleeding!"

Ava brought her hand to her forehead. It was slippery with blood. "I'm fine." But as soon as the words left her mouth, everything began to spin.

"Here." Tess grabbed her arm, steering her toward a nearby bench and drawing her down to sit on it. "Are you sure you're okay?"

"I'm fine. Just need to catch my breath."

"I can't believe you did that. You just threw yourself at her. She had a gun. She could have killed you!"

"What have I been telling you all along? I said I'd protect you, and I did. Not because of any promise I made. Not because I felt guilty. But because of how I feel about you."

She took Tess's hand in hers, holding it firmly.

"Since the night we met, I've lied to you. I've pushed you away. I've been selfish, pretending I was doing these things to protect you, when really, I was trying to protect myself. Because I didn't want to fall for you. I didn't want to fall for anyone, but you? You made me feel things I've never felt before, feelings so strong that they scared me. Love doesn't come easy to me. But with you, it has."

Tess stared back at Ava, her lips parting with a soft breath. "Are you saying you…"

"Yes. I love you, Tess. I want to be with you. I want you to be mine, but not in the way you've been mine before. I want your heart. And I want to give you mine in return."

"Ava…" Tess's eyes sparkled with tears. "I want that too. I want that more than anything. I love you."

Ava kissed her gently. But not a second after their lips met, they were interrupted by footsteps. Ava sprang to her feet, ready to protect Tess from this new threat.

But it was only Riley. They hurried toward the bench,

their usually impassive face marked with concern. "Are you all right? I heard gunshots."

Ava nodded. "We're fine. I took care of it."

Riley glanced at Julie on the ground before returning her attention to Ava. "You're hurt."

"I'm all right. Just a little dizzy."

Her head was still ringing from when Julie had smashed it against the stone. And with the adrenaline of the encounter wearing off, fatigue was taking hold, the world around her turning fuzzy.

"Looks like a concussion," Riley said. "You shouldn't be on your feet."

"I'm fine," Ava protested. Nevertheless, Tess urged Ava down onto the bench again.

"An ambulance is on the way," Riley said. "So are the police. Tess, keep an eye on her while I take care of Julie."

They pulled some zip ties from a pocket in their jacket and fastened them securely around the unconscious woman's wrists. As Tess fussed over Ava, Ava glanced at the large statutes placed strategically around the courtyard garden. Several of them hid cameras and microphones.

"Did you check the cameras?" she asked Riley.

"As soon as we get you patched up, I'll take a look," Riley replied. "But I'm sure they got everything."

"She confessed. I made sure she confessed to it all. You need to give the recordings to the police."

Riley nodded. "I will."

Ava turned back to Tess and took her hand, squeezing it gently.

"It's over," she said. "Julie is going away where she can't hurt you. You're safe now."

"Oh, Ava," Tess said. "I was always safe with you."

A smile pulled at Ava's lips. "Did I tell you how much I love you?"

"Yes, you did. I love you too."

Tess's words were the last thing Ava heard as the world around her faded. She closed her eyes, secure in the knowledge that she'd finally fulfilled her promise.

CHAPTER 28

"For the last time, I'm *fine*."

From her seat on the living room couch, Ava gave Tess a glare that stopped her in her tracks. She'd only offered to bring Ava something to eat.

For the third time that day. After Ava had told her to stop asking.

Perhaps she was being a little overbearing.

"I'm sorry," she said. "I'm just trying to help."

"It was just a concussion. And that was *weeks* ago."

"Two weeks," Tess corrected her.

Ava crossed her arms. "Yes, and I've spent the entire time letting you boss me around and treat me like I'm at death's door."

"Only because you keep insisting on doing everything yourself instead of resting like the doctor told you to."

"Well, according to the doctor, I've fully recovered. I assure you, I'm fine now. All this fussing over me is completely unnecessary!"

"All right, I'll stop." Tess sat down next to her. "And just so you know, I don't mind fussing over you. It's been kind of nice to take care of *you* for once. Plus, I have to repay you for saving my life."

"You don't have to repay me for anything. I did what I did because I love you."

"And I'll always be grateful to you for that." Tess kissed her on the cheek before running her finger across the scar on Ava's forehead. "Looks like this has finally healed."

"It looked far worse than it was," Ava grumbled.

Nevertheless, Tess found it reassuring. All their wounds were healed. All loose ends tied up. Everything behind them now.

Well, almost everything. Julie was in jail, still awaiting trial. But with her actions in the courtyard that day caught on video, along with her confession that she'd hired hitmen to kill Tess, the case against her was solid. All of Julie's connections and whatever money she had left couldn't get her out of serving a lengthy prison sentence. They didn't have to worry about her anymore.

The icing on the cake? Ava had hired the best lawyers in the country to make sure Tess got her inheritance. Soon, she'd have more money than she knew what to do with. She'd be set for life.

But what did money matter when Tess had everything she could possibly want right in front of her?

She let out a contented sigh. "I'm just glad we can finally put this behind us and move on with our lives."

"So am I," Ava said. "I'm looking forward to starting a new life with you."

"Oh? Because I know you said you wanted to be with

me, but that was right after you hit your head. Did you really mean it, or was that the concussion talking?"

While Tess's words had been playful, Ava's expression remained serious. "I meant it. I meant it with all my heart." She took Tess's hand in both of hers, holding it firmly. "I never thought that sharing my life with someone—*building* a life with someone—was something I'd want. But with you, I want that more than anything."

Tess's heart fluttered. But before she could say a word, Riley appeared in the living room doorway, a large duffel bag slung over one shoulder, sunglasses perched on their head of raven-black hair.

"Just letting you know I'm all packed to go," Riley said.

Ava rose from her seat. "We've kept you here long enough. Thank you for everything. We appreciate it."

"Just doing my job. But I'm always happy to help. And I'm happy you two found each other."

Warmth rose up Tess's face. Did Ava have any idea of the subtle part her 'driver' had played in pushing them together?

Riley gave them both a nod. "If you need me, you know where to find me. But I hope you don't need my services again. For your sakes."

They said their farewells, Ava and Riley sharing a brief embrace. Then Riley turned and left the room, their footsteps receding down the hallway.

Ava sat back down and took Tess's hand again. "Now, where were we?"

"Well, you were just telling me about how excited you are to build a new life with me," Tess said. "And I was about to tell you how wonderful that sounds."

"Then let's start now. I want you to move in with me. Here, on the island."

Tess smiled. "I'd love that. But I was also thinking, when I get my inheritance, I want to buy us an apartment in the city so we can spend more time there. I want to do all the things I've always wanted to do, like go to college. And that's going to be hard if we're always holed up here. Don't get me wrong. I love it here, and I want this to be our home. But for me, home is wherever you are."

Ava squeezed Tess's hand. "Say no more. I want you to be happy, to have the life you've always dreamed of. Besides, I've kept myself locked up in the mansion for too long. I think it's time I started living my life, too."

Tess leaned over to plant a grateful kiss on Ava's lips. Ava drew her into her arms, her body pressed against Tess's. Tess murmured into her lips, desire rising inside her. With Ava's injuries and the aftermath of the confrontation with Julie, their lives had been so hectic that they'd barely had time for more than a kiss here and there. Tess ached for Ava's touch, her unique brand of intimacy. It had only been two weeks, but it felt like so, *so* long.

She broke off the kiss, drawing a hand down Ava's arm. "How about we take this to the bedroom so we can *really* celebrate the start of our life together?"

"Isn't that a wonderful idea?" Ava said. "But after two whole weeks of you bossing me around and forcing me to rest, all in the name of taking care of me?"

Tess's heart began to race. All of a sudden, Ava was looking at her like she was her prey.

She leaned in close, forcing Tess back against the arm of the couch. "We're going to do it my way."

"How I've missed this." Ava took Tess's chin in her fingers, tilting her head up to face her own. "Having you down here with me, in your rightful place."

A shiver rolled along Tess's body. She and Ava were back in the basement, and they were finally making use of some of the specialized furniture in it.

Namely, what Ava referred to as a bondage horse. It was obvious why. The long bench was covered in padding and leather, with two A-frames at either end, like some kind of kinky sawhorse.

And Tess? She was bent over it, lying along the bench with her feet on the floor. Her ankles were tied to the legs of the A, holding them apart, her wrists were bound together and tied off to the 'head' of the horse.

She was immobilized. Powerless. And while she wasn't naked, the only clothing she had on was the loose summer dress she'd been lounging around the house in. She'd removed her panties at Ava's instruction before she tied her up.

Tess hadn't asked why, but she was sure it had to do with the leather paddle Ava was holding.

"And now that I have you in your rightful place, I can introduce you to another of my favorite tools." She released Tess's chin, drawing the paddle through her hand lovingly. "See how thin and supple it is? That means it has more bite. Almost like a whip."

Ava slapped the paddle against her palm, the sharp crack that rang through the air jolting Tess's body. Her heart pounded, along with the arousal pulsing between her legs.

"Pain is the finest of delicacies. Just the smallest amount can bring the sweetest release." Ava dragged the paddle along the back of Tess's neck and the length of her spine. "But I'm feeling generous this evening. And sometimes, we have to allow ourselves to indulge. Sometimes, we have to be a little naughty." She leaned down, her body pressing against Tess's back as she spoke softly into her ear. "So, do you want a taste?"

Tess quivered. "Yes."

Ava drew the paddle up Tess's thigh, pushing up the hem of her dress to draw slow circles around her bare ass cheek. "That was hardly convincing. You can do better."

Tess bit back a groan. This was torture! "Please, Ava. Show me. Use me as you desire."

"That's what I like to hear, my love. You're *mine*. To take. To use. To cherish. And to toy with."

The paddle disappeared from Tess's skin. She squeezed her eyes shut, waiting for it to fall.

As if in slow motion, Ava brought the paddle down, striking the tender flesh of Tess's ass. She cried out, shock and desire flooding her in equal measure. It didn't feel the same as when Ava had used the whip on her the very first night in the basement. The paddle was more solid, more impactful. But it stung all the same.

Ava struck her again, once, twice, three times, with ever-increasing force. And each time, she murmured with satisfaction at the sounds Tess made, at her body's reactions. The perverse pleasure Ava took in pushing her to her limits only made Tess hotter.

But even more, it warmed her heart to know she'd found

someone as delightfully twisted as herself to share her life with.

"That's it," Ava crooned, gliding her hands over Tess's stinging skin. "Tell me how much you love this. Tell me you want more."

"Please," Tess whispered, breathless. "*More.*"

Ava obliged, bringing down the paddle over Tess's bare ass and thighs over and over, each strike on her tender flesh sending shockwaves through her. Of pain and pleasure. Of anticipation and need. Of every sensation imaginable, until she was floating in a sea of euphoria.

Which was why she barely noticed Ava had stopped until her lips were on Tess's, her hands stroking Tess's face. "That felt good, didn't it?"

Tess purred. Her whole body was alight, burning for Ava.

A hint of a smile crossed Ava's lips. "I'm not done with you yet. Don't go anywhere."

She disappeared from Tess's view, and her awareness. Tess didn't realize she'd returned until she felt Ava's hands on her thighs and cheeks, soothing her tender skin. And when she slid a hand between Tess's outspread legs, it was like a bolt of electricity straight to her core.

Ava traced her finger over Tess's clit. "You've been such a good toy. You deserve to be rewarded."

Ava's hand disappeared. Tess let out an involuntary groan. But it was cut short when something hard probed between her legs.

The heat of anticipation rushed through Tess's body. She pushed her hips back, toward Ava and the strap-on she wore. But restrained as she was, Tess could barely move at all.

She whimpered. In her hyper-sensitized state, words were beyond her. But she didn't have to say a single thing. Her need was written all over her body.

And Ava could see it. Slowly, she slipped the tip of the strap-on between Tess's lower lips and eased inside, burying herself deep. Tess's gasp turned into a moan as Ava grabbed hold of her hips and began to thrust, her slow, deliberate strokes sending pleasure shooting through Tess's body.

Yes. Take me. Use me. Cherish me. Ava's sweet words echoed in her mind. Tess was hers, wholly and completely.

And when Ava took up the paddle again, striking Tess on the side of the ass as she thrust inside, the last of the control she still had over herself crumbled.

"Oh god," she gasped. "Oh, Ava!"

A few more strikes were all it took to send Tess hurtling past the point of no return. She cried out as a climax ripped through her, shattering her body. She quaked against the padded bench, her limbs pulling vainly at their restraints. But Ava didn't stop rocking her hips, didn't stop striking tender flesh and caressing Tess's skin with soothing hands, until she'd ridden the wave of ecstasy to its peak and back down again.

She lay against the bench, dazed and breathless. As Tess regained her senses, Ava freed her from her bonds and gathered her into her arms. Tess murmured blissfully as Ava painted kisses on her lips, only stopping to draw Tess over to the bed at the other end of the room.

Off went Tess's dress, pulled over her head by Ava. Ava's own dress followed, along with her bra and panties.

Both naked now, they collapsed onto the bed, a tangle of limbs and lust. As Ava's hands traveled lovingly over Tess's body, Tess did the same, exploring Ava's curves, relishing her soft skin, adoring every inch of her. The strap-on was long gone, the silken heat between Ava's legs calling to her.

Would Ava let Tess touch her like that? It was so decidedly vanilla compared to everything they'd done together. But it required a vulnerability from Ava that she'd never given Tess before.

Ava pulled back, her eyes searching Tess's. "What is it?"

"I..." Tess bit her lower lip. "I want to touch you. Taste you. May I? Please?"

For a moment, she was sure Ava would say no, would push her down to the bed and ravish her with pleasure until she forgot what she'd even asked.

Instead, she cupped Tess's cheek in her hand. "Yes, my love. Show me your devotion to me."

Tess slipped from her grasp and trailed her lips downward, down Ava's neck, her shoulders, her chest. She kissed Ava's breasts and nipples, one after the other, her mouth and tongue teasing and sucking.

Soft breaths fell from Ava's lips as she arched into Tess's mouth, silently spurring her on. She traced a hand up to the peak of Ava's thighs, skimming a finger up between her lower lips. She was warm and wet, and oh so inviting.

"Yes..." Ava pushed down on Tess's shoulders, her head rolling back. "Taste me."

Tess slid down her body, positioning herself between Ava's outspread legs, and dipped her head between them, snaking her tongue over Ava's silken folds. Tess was still drunk from her orgasm, and Ava's sweet scent, the heat of her against her lips and the taste of her on her tongue only intoxicated Tess more.

Ava's hands fell to Tess's head to guide her. "Yes, like that. Devour me. Worship me."

Yes, Ava. She was a goddess. Tess was her servant, eager and willing. She wrapped her arms around Ava's thighs, holding on tightly as she devoured her. She glided her tongue up and down the length of Ava's slit, circling her clit, darting into her entrance. And when she found that sensitive spot just below Ava's swollen bud that made her shudder and moan, she honed in on it, strumming and sucking, rolling and licking with wild abandon.

Soon, Ava began trembling uncontrollably, her thighs squeezing around Tess's head. A few more strokes of her tongue were enough to send Ava over the edge. Her hips rose from the bed, arching into Tess as a cry flew from her, echoing through the basement. Tess didn't stop until Ava slumped back down to the mattress, breathing hard.

As she pried herself out from between Ava's legs, Ava drew her up to kiss her.

"Thank you," Tess murmured once Ava allowed her to breathe again. "For letting me have that."

"My love." Ava caressed the side of Tess's face. "Whatever you want is yours. I've told you that before, and I'll tell you again. If you want me—*all* of me—I'll give you that. I'm yours."

Tess closed her eyes and settled against Ava's chest, letting the silence embrace them. *If I could lie here for all eternity, I would.*

They didn't have eternity. But they did have a lifetime.

Ava broke the silence. "I once promised I'd protect you. Now, I want to make a new promise."

Tess looked up at her. "What is it?"

Ava wrapped her arms around her, drawing her closer. "I promise you'll always be mine. And that I'll never, ever let you go."

EPILOGUE 1

Tess stared wide-eyed at the woman walking by. "Is that who I think it is?" she whispered.

Ava nodded. "Madison Sloane." The lesbian media magnate was nowhere near the most famous member of the Queens Club, but as the founder of an international media empire, she was certainly one of the most influential.

Ava exchanged a greeting with her, but when she attempted to introduce Madison to Tess, Tess stumbled over her words.

"Should I be jealous?" Ava murmured once the woman was out of earshot.

Tess's cheeks flushed. "Of course not. I'm just not used to being around anyone so famous. But none of the women here compare to you. None of the women in the entire world do."

The two of them had stopped by the Queens Club for dinner and were now enjoying drinks in the bar. It was the first time Ava had brought Tess to the private club. Although guests were allowed, the exclusive nature of the club meant that anyone who stepped through the doors had to be thoroughly vetted by Cassandra and made to sign various agreements, including an NDA.

It was often more trouble than it was worth, which was why Ava hadn't brought Tess to the club sooner. But after a year together, it was time to bring her into the fold, to share the last part of her life Ava had kept secret from her.

And soon, Ava would ask her to commit to sharing a life with her forever.

She resisted the urge to check her purse for the ring contained within it. She'd made plans for a grand proposal during their upcoming anniversary trip. It wasn't for another week, but she'd been carrying the ring around with her for weeks to keep Tess from stumbling upon it.

And perhaps a small part of her kept it with her out of anxiety. Ava had made business deals that put half her fortune at risk without batting an eyelid. She'd charged at an armed madwoman intent on murdering her and Tess without a second thought.

But asking the love of her life to be hers forever? Ava couldn't think of anything more nerve-racking.

And she couldn't think of anything she wanted more.

Tess tilted her head, studying Ava. "Is something on your mind?"

Ava took a sip of her martini. "Not at all. I'm simply thinking about how lovely it is to spend time with friends. And with the woman I love."

Tess smiled. "I'm having a nice time too. And I can't believe half the people I've seen here tonight. Who knew there was a club like this hidden right here in the middle of the city? It's like some kind of secret society."

"It's nothing sinister, I assure you."

"Well, it's still pretty amazing." Tess glanced around the room, then did a double-take. "Is that... Riley? What are they doing here?"

Riley turned at the sound of their name. Spotting Ava and Tess, they waved and approached the table, offering a warm greeting.

"It's been a while," Riley said. "Good to see you."

"Likewise," Ava replied. "You've been busy, it seems."

"You know how it is. My services are in high demand." They looked from Ava to Tess and back again. "How about you two? I hope your lives have quieted down a little since I last saw you."

"Compared to a year ago, our lives have been utterly mundane." Ava gestured toward the empty chair across the table. "Why don't you take a seat? We'll tell you all about it."

"Another time," Riley said. "I need to get going. I only dropped by to talk to Cassandra about some club business."

Club business? Riley was being deliberately vague. Was something going on?

They said their farewells. As soon as Riley was gone, Tess spoke up.

"Wait, so Riley is a member of the Queens Club?"

Ava nodded. "That's right."

"Didn't you say that membership is only for important or powerful people? Are we still pretending Riley is just a driver?"

"Driving *is* one of their skills. Among many." Ava left it at that. It wasn't her place to divulge Riley's background. And in all honesty, she knew very little about it. "Now, about our anniversary trip. Everything is booked, and I managed to move some meetings around so we can squeeze in a couple of extra nights. We'll be back just before the semester starts."

"That sounds perfect. I can't wait." Tess sipped her cocktail, gazing up at Ava from underneath dark eyelashes. "So, are you going to tell me where we're going?"

"No, because that would ruin the surprise." Their destination was a luxury villa in Spain, but Ava wanted to keep Tess on her toes to distract her from the *real* surprise. "You'll find out when we get there."

Tess huffed.

"Now, don't pout at me like that." Ava leaned in close, dropping her voice low. "And if you ask me again, when we get home, I'll take you down to the basement and spank you. And then I won't let you come until our trip."

Tess's entire face turned pink. Ava would never grow tired of how easy it was to get her all worked up. Perhaps it was time for the two of them to go somewhere more private—

"Ava."

Cassandra's voice. Ava turned to see her approaching their table, her expression more solemn than usual.

"Sorry to interrupt, Tess, but I need to speak to Ava in private," she said. "It won't take long."

Ava nodded. After assuring Tess she'd be right back, she rose to her feet and followed Cassandra out of the bar. But the woman didn't take her into one of the empty rooms nearby. She went all the way up to her office.

And she didn't say a word until they were inside it, the door shut firmly behind her.

"What's going on?" Ava asked. "Is something the matter?"

"I'll cut to the chase. I've been getting my affairs in order, and I've decided that if anything happens to me, or I'm unable to run the Queens Club, I want you to take over. I'm leaving it to you."

"Cass, I don't know what to say. I'm touched that you'd entrust the club to me. But what brought this on? Is everything all right?"

"Everything is fine. I'm just taking precautions."

Ava searched Cassandra's eyes. "I know something is wrong. If something is going on, tell me. You *know* you can trust me."

"I do. But this is something I need to handle on my own."

"Why? Is it to do with the Queens Club? Is it why Riley was here? Are you in some kind of trouble?"

"I have it all under control," Cassandra said.

"You have what under control? Talk to me."

Cassandra looked away for a moment. When she met Ava's eyes again, they were filled with cold, hard resolve. And something else.

Fear.

Her hands curled into fists at her sides. "It's my past. It's finally caught up with me."

EPILOGUE 2

Tess sipped at her cocktail, gazing around at the room as she waited for Ava to return. She was trying her hardest not to stare at any of the famous faces around her. Ava had trusted her enough to bring her to this secret club. She wasn't going to ruin things by acting like an awestruck tourist.

She set her drink down, letting her mind wander to their upcoming trip. A whole week of just the two of them together, somewhere far away and new? She couldn't wait.

Not that their everyday lives were boring. Tess was living the life of her dreams. She and Ava split their days between the island mansion and the penthouse apartment in the city whenever Tess had classes. The apartment was the one thing she'd splurged on after receiving her inheritance, and it was worth every penny.

She'd also bought a few gifts for Ava, but she'd squirreled the rest of the money away for the future. She didn't know what the future would bring. But she was certain she wanted to spend it with Ava.

She let out a wistful sigh. *A future with Ava. Spending the rest of our lives together.* Was it crazy to think like that, after only a year together? But their relationship had always been fast. Intense. Passionate.

No, Tess didn't need any more time to know that she wanted to spend the rest of her days by Ava's side. She already knew it in her heart. The two of them shared a bond that couldn't be broken, a connection that couldn't be severed.

Which was why she was only slightly concerned about Ava's unusual behavior over the past few weeks. She seemed preoccupied, even a little furtive. But it had to be because of the surprise anniversary trip she was planning. Tess had no reason to worry. After all, she trusted Ava.

She reached for her drink. But in a moment of clumsiness, she knocked it over, spilling it across the table.

She cursed and grabbed a napkin, attempting to mop up the spill. But the drink had dripped over the edge of the table and onto her shoe. As she leaned over to wipe it off, she saw Ava's purse on the floor by her chair. The spill had reached it too.

Tess cursed again, this time attracting a few stares. She grabbed another napkin to clean off the leather purse. As she attempted to wipe up the liquid that had trickled inside it, she spotted a small, unfamiliar velvet box among the contents of the purse.

Without thinking, she pulled the box out and opened it up. Inside was a white gold ring encrusted with diamonds.

Hm? What is this?

The realization hit her like a crashing wave. Was this why Ava had been acting so strangely?

Because she was going to propose?

Anxious excitement fluttered in her belly. Ava was going to propose!

And Tess had ruined the surprise!

She snapped the ring box shut and stuffed it back in Ava's purse, setting it down on the table, her pulse racing.

And just in time, because Ava chose that moment to return.

She slid into the seat next to Tess. "Is everything all right?"

Tess nodded. "I just spilled my drink, that's all."

Ava surveyed the damage. "Let's get that cleaned up. And get you another drink."

She caught the eye of a passing server. Within seconds, the spill had been wiped up, another cocktail on the way.

Ava sat back in her chair. "There. All better."

Tess nodded, too flustered to speak.

"Are you sure you're okay?"

"I'm fine," she squeaked.

Ava fixed her eyes on Tess. "Be honest with me. I've already had to drag the truth out of one person tonight. I'll do it again."

Tess's stomach flipped. There was no resisting Ava's intense gaze. There was no keeping anything from her.

She had to come clean.

"Well, I…" She glanced at Ava's purse. "When I spilled my drink, it went everywhere. Including on your purse. *In* your purse, too."

Understanding dawned on Ava's face. "Ah. I'm guessing you took a look inside?"

"Not on purpose! I was trying to clean it up, and I—"

"And you saw it?"

Tess nodded. "I'm sorry."

"It's fine," Ava reached for her purse and took the ring box out of it. "I was planning to do this on our trip, but since the cat's out of the bag, why wait?"

Tess froze. "W-what do you mean?"

She watched in stunned silence as Ava stood up, smoothed down her dress, and took Tess's hand, drawing her to her feet.

"Ava…" Tess looked around the room and then back at her. "Are you…"

"Yes. I am."

Without hesitation, Ava got down on one knee and opened up the box, presenting the ring to her.

"Tess Bennett, will you do me the honor of becoming my wife?"

Tess's heart surged. She was so overcome with joy that she almost forgot to answer Ava's question.

"Yes," she said. "Yes, I'll marry you."

Ava rose to her feet and pulled Tess into her arms. As they shared a kiss, applause broke out around them. Tess hadn't noticed that they'd gained an audience. As far as she was concerned, she and Ava were the only two people in the world.

An eternity passed before Ava broke off the kiss, but she didn't let go of her. "What do you say we leave for our trip a few days early? To celebrate our engagement."

"I'd love that," Tess replied. "And I'll make up for ruining the surprise on the trip, I promise."

Ava gave her a firm but sultry look, lowering her voice

so that only Tess could hear it. "Oh, I'll make sure you do. Believe me."

A smile pulled at Tess's lips. She expected nothing less from Ava.

She finally had everything she'd ever wanted. Someone who loved her. Someone who cherished her. Someone to call home.

She had everything her heart desired right here in her arms.

ABOUT THE AUTHOR

Anna Stone is the author of lesbian romance bestsellers Being Hers, Tangled Vows, and more. Her sizzling sapphic romances feature strong, passionate women who love women. In every one of her books, you'll find off-the-charts heat and a guaranteed happily ever after.
Anna lives in Australia with her girlfriend and their cat. When she isn't writing, she can usually be found with a coffee in one hand and a book in the other.

Visit **annastoneauthor.com** to find out more about her books and to sign up for her newsletter.

Printed in Great Britain
by Amazon

16779480R00137